W9-CDH-702

Ryan Quinn and the
Lion's Claw

ALSO BY RON McGEE

Ryan Quinn and the Rebel's Escape

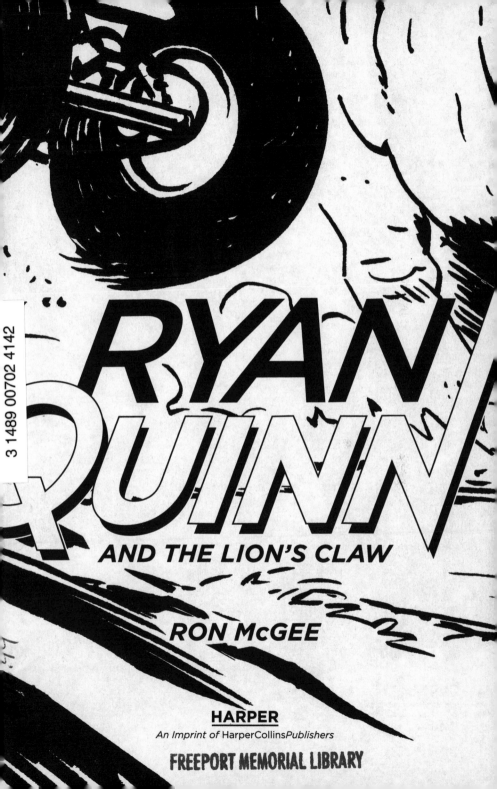

RYAN QUINN

AND THE LION'S CLAW

RON McGEE

HARPER

An Imprint of HarperCollins Publishers

Library of Congress Cataloging-in-Publication Data
Names: McGee, Ron, author. | Samnee, Chris, illustrator.
Title: Ryan Quinn and the lion's claw / by Ron McGee ;
    illustrated by Chris Samnee.
Description: First Edition. | New York : Harper, an imprint of
    HarperCollinsPublishersCollins, 2017. | Series: Ryan Quinn
    ; [2] | Summary: Ryan Quinn and his best friend, Danny,
    stowaway on a plane to Africa in an attempt to save
    two revolutionary musicians whose identities have been
    compromised by a traitor within the Emegency Rescue
    Committee, while Ryan's parents, and ERC operatives, try to
    track the turncoat back in New York.
Identifiers: LCCN 2016054190 | ISBN 978-0-06-242169-2
    (hardback)
Subjects: | CYAC: Secret societies--Fiction. | Blacks--Africa--
    Fiction. | Africa--Fiction. | Adventure and adventurers--
    Fiction. | BISAC: JUVENILE FICTION / Action & Adventure
    / General.
Classification: LCC PZ7.1.M43514 Ry 2017 | DDC [Fic]--dc23 LC
    record available at https://lccn.loc.gov/2016054190

Book design by Victor Joseph Ochoa
17 18 19 20 21   CG/LSCH   10 9 8 7 6 5 4 3 2 1

First Edition

Adventures are more fun when you
share them with good friends. Luckily
for me, I've got some of the greatest!
This book is dedicated to them.

—RM

PROLOGUE

**NEW JERSEY,
USA**

*T*he music would get them both killed.

That's what Lawrence always told her, and he was probably right. But without the music, everything felt empty and point-less. How do you stop doing the one thing that makes you feel truly alive?

Nadia didn't have much time. Lawrence would be home soon, and she wanted to get the last track recorded before he arrived. She had written the new song earlier today during her shift at the Coffee Hut. The lyrics and melody just popped into her head while she made dou-ble mocha lattes and nonfat cappuccinos. Every time she got a break, Nadia scribbled notes to herself before she forgot.

The song was almost finished. She hadn't felt this excited in years. Growing up, music was often her only refuge from a frightening and dangerous world. It was Lawrence who eventually showed Nadia that her voice could be much more than an escape.

It could be a weapon.

And for a while, it had been. But that was years ago. Now she spent her days serving coffee and her nights safely tucked away in this drab little apartment. She tried to make the best of it, but this place would never feel like home.

So once again, music had become her refuge.

The recording would be simple. All she had was a laptop, an electric keyboard, and a beat-up microphone she'd bought at a pawnshop. She put on headphones, then pressed record. A hip-hop beat played. Nadia took a deep breath, leaned into the microphone, and—

The front door of the apartment burst open! The lock splintered with explosive force as two men in black rushed into the room. Nadia screamed and bolted for the back door.

She grabbed the edge of an empty table and yanked it into the path of her pursuers. They barely slowed, leaping it effortlessly. She whirled around the corner and raced through the kitchen. Nadia flung open the back door . . . and stopped short.

A pistol with a silencer was pointed at her chest. She recognized the man holding it. She'd never forget the horrible scar that stretched across his eye and cheek.

"Hello, doll." His elegant British accent didn't mask the menace in his tone. "I know someone who's gonna be very pleased to see you again."

Nadia spun around but found her way blocked by one of the other men. She wouldn't let them take her! She lunged forward with a guttural roar, swiping her long nails across his cheek.

The man staggered back in surprise. Nadia pushed past him, but before she could take another step, she felt a blow to the back of her head. Dropping to her knees, she struggled to focus. But the room was spinning, everything blurry.

Nadia's last thought was for Lawrence, a prayer that they wouldn't get him, too. Then she tumbled to the ground, blackness enveloping her.

PART ONE

SIDELINED

CHAPTER
01

**NEW YORK,
USA**

Heads up, Quinn!"

Ryan pivoted to discover Brendan Jackson making a fast break toward the basket. Ryan mentally kicked himself. He'd been distracted again, his mind wandering.

Ryan tried to catch up, but he was too late. Jackson bounded toward the backboard and executed a perfect layup. Two points.

"Come on, Quinn!" Coach Harris yelled. "Stop daydreaming or get off the court!"

Ryan nodded, frustrated and embarrassed. Baseball was his passion, but that didn't start until spring, so he'd tried out for the travel basketball team. He made the team because he was pretty athletic, but he was seriously lacking in basic skills. Ryan wanted to get better, and that would require him to keep his mind on the game.

For the next half hour, Ryan forced himself not to think about anything but practice. Not about his parents, not about the Emergency Rescue Committee—he focused on getting rebounds, setting screens, and making jump shots.

And it worked. When he concentrated on the game, Ryan was good. He even made a sweet three-pointer at the end of practice. As the players left the court, Coach Harris came up beside him.

"You want to be here, Quinn?" he asked.

"Yes, sir. Absolutely."

"You've got natural talent. But basketball's a mental game." Coach Harris stopped, serious. "When you're out there, everything else has to go away. Algebra tests, that girl you think is cute, the fight you had with your mom this morning. I don't care what the problem is, you leave it outside my gym."

Ryan wished his problems were that simple. Less than four weeks ago, his whole world had changed. He'd watched his mom get kidnapped and had been forced to abandon his injured father in a dangerous country thousands of miles from home. The discovery that his parents were part of the Emergency Rescue Committee had stunned Ryan. Operating secretly for decades, ERC operatives risked their lives rescuing people around the world who were being persecuted and silenced for speaking out against oppression and tyranny. Mom and Dad had been leading a whole cloak-and-dagger life that Ryan knew nothing about until a month ago.

Part of Ryan was proud of his parents and the work they did. But he felt hurt and angry, too. Why hadn't they trusted him with the truth? Were they *ever* planning to tell him?

Of course, he couldn't say any of this to the coach. He knew excuses wouldn't matter, anyway. "I got it, Coach. Won't happen again."

Coach Harris smiled. "That's what I wanna hear."

As they headed out of the gym, Ryan saw his friend Danny on the bleachers. "Dude! You done?"

Danny's wild hair was spiked out in more directions than usual today. A vintage leather bomber jacket covered his concert T-shirt, this one from New Order's 1988 European tour. Danny was always a bundle of energy, but the last few weeks he'd been bouncing off the walls.

"You're not gonna believe what I found." Danny joined Ryan.

"Let me guess," Ryan said. "Some poor person in a far-off place who desperately needs rescuing?" Since learning about the ERC and helping with Ryan's first mission, Danny had been searching for some way to get involved again.

"Well, yeah," Danny admitted. "But this guy really needs us! He's been locked up in a North Korean prison for, like, twenty years—just for leading a student protest."

"And how exactly are we supposed to break into a North Korean prison?" Ryan admired Danny's passion, but this was the fourth prisoner of conscience he'd brought up this week.

Danny shrugged. "It's not like I've figured out the entire plan yet or anything."

"You know what my parents said. No way they're letting us get involved in another ERC mission."

"But that's so unfair," Danny said. "It's not like anything that bad happened."

"You got *stabbed*," Ryan pointed out. "And I got shot at. A lot."

Danny sighed. "Sure, take their side."

The truth was, Ryan felt the same as Danny.

Since his adventure in Andakar, he felt like he was missing out on something pretty much all the time.

"I'm gonna head over to the library and study for the physical science midterm," Ryan said. "Wanna come?"

"I guess." Danny fell into step beside Ryan, heading back toward the school. "But you gotta admit, planning a jailbreak in North Korea sounds like a lot more fun."

CHAPTER 02

**NEW YORK,
USA**

New York City in winter was even better than Ryan had hoped. The brisk December air seemed to energize everyone. Bundled in coats and scarves, people were in a festive mood. Decorations were hung everywhere you looked. This would be his family's first holiday season in their new home, and Ryan's parents were determined to make it special.

In the last two weeks alone, they'd gone to see *The Nutcracker* ballet, checked out amazing window displays at department stores, and now they were ice-skating at Rockefeller Center. The biggest Christmas tree Ryan had ever seen towered over them. It was all really touristy, but fun, since he still felt kind of like a tourist. Mom and Dad were trying hard to make it seem like life was "normal" after everything that had happened.

"Out of the way, slowpoke!" Ryan turned as his friend Kasey zipped by, speeding past him even though she was skating *backward*. Kasey's wild hair was tucked behind a pair of fuzzy purple earmuffs, her cheeks red from the chafing wind. She made skating look so easy. "Look out!"

Ryan turned just in time to keep from plowing right into the back of a little kid. Skating really wasn't his thing, and the abrupt stop made him lose his balance. Ryan toppled to the freezing ice as Kasey glided over.

"Sorry," she said. "You okay?"

Ryan grinned. "Show-off."

"I spent five years doing competitive figure skating." Kasey reached out, helping Ryan stand back up. "I'm more at home on the ice than just about anywhere."

"So why'd you stop?"

"You get to this point where you have to give it one hundred percent dedication if you want to win. Skating has to be your whole life. I have too many other things I'm interested in."

The more Ryan got to know Kasey, the better he liked her. She was curious about everything, always asking questions about the places he'd lived and wanting to talk about what was going on in the world. They'd been hanging out constantly for a few weeks now and never ran out of things to talk about. And she really was crazy cute.

"Do I have something on my face?" Kasey asked.

"What? No."

"Then why are you staring at me like that?"

Ryan was saved from answering by the arrival of his mom and dad, holding hands as they skidded to a stop. "Hey, you two, who's up for hot chocolate?"

Looking at John and Jacqueline Quinn no one would guess they were part of a supersecret covert organization. They looked like regular parents—even a little dorky in their matching striped beanies with the giant pom-poms on top. Mom wanted Ryan to wear one, too, but so far he'd managed to escape that humiliation.

Since learning about the ERC, Ryan had pummeled his parents with a million questions. But they were insistent that he was too young to be working with the group and the less he knew, the safer he'd be. It was incredibly frustrating.

They tried to act like everything was the way it used to be. But it wasn't.

"Why don't we go to La Maison du Chocolat?" his mom suggested as the four of them skated off the rink. Having been raised in France, Jacqueline was even more of a chocolate connoisseur than Ryan, and La Maison made some of the best in the world. Normally, he would have been excited to go. But Ryan couldn't shake the feeling that all this activity was just to keep him from asking more questions they didn't want to answer.

Mom and Dad had been acting weird the last couple of days, whispering intently when they thought he wasn't paying attention. Even their suggestion to invite Kasey to join them tonight felt like another way to keep from talking about anything important.

Jacqueline squeezed Ryan's arm. "We could get a few of those fantastic chocolate pralines, too."

"Sounds great." He gave her a reassuring smile as they sat on the benches to take off their skates.

Kasey plopped down beside him. "What's wrong?"

They hadn't known each other that long, but already she could read his moods. Ryan glanced at his parents, making sure they couldn't hear. "I think there's something new going on. Something they don't want me to know about."

"About the ERC?" Kasey knew all about the Emergency Rescue Committee. Her help last month had proved invaluable. But unlike Danny, she knew how to keep a secret and didn't talk about it unless Ryan brought it up.

"It has to be the ERC. It's so annoying—they're still keeping things from me, only now I *know* it."

"Give them time." She picked up her skates. "Come on, some hot chocolate will make you forget all about it."

Ryan doubted that was true. They joined his parents, finding Mom and Dad staring at his dad's cell phone, reading something with troubled expressions.

"Everything okay?" Ryan asked.

Dad quickly clicked the cell phone off as they both looked up. His mom's smile was immediate, but Ryan could tell it was fake.

"Fine," she said, getting up. "This was fun, wasn't it? Maybe we should go see the *Radio City Christmas Spectacular* this weekend. We could invite Danny, too. Kasey, have you ever seen the Rockettes?"

As his mom walked past to join Kasey, Ryan stopped his father. "Dad, what's going on?"

For a moment, Ryan saw the hesitation in his father's eyes and thought he might actually tell him. But Dad finally forced a weak smile. "Nothing you need to worry about."

He tousled Ryan's mop of hair affectionately, then put an arm around his shoulder as they headed out.

Ryan knew he was right. Something was wrong, and they weren't telling him what it was. The last time he'd been left in the dark, he had almost lost both his mom and his dad. He wasn't about to let that happen again.

Which meant he'd have to find out what was really going on some other way.

CHAPTER
03

**NEW YORK,
USA**

D ad, hold on!"
Ryan leaned over the cliff, reaching
out to his father. Dad hung to a rock
outcropping, his fingers slipping a little more
every second. Down below, the canyon went on
forever, disappearing into an endless black hole.

Ryan grabbed his dad's wrist and pulled. His
father dangled, legs twisting in the air, struggling helplessly to find a toehold.

"Don't let go," Dad pleaded.

"I won't—I promise." But Ryan was losing
the battle. He couldn't pull his dad back up. He
wasn't strong enough.

"Ryan, I'm counting on you. You have to
save me!"

"I'm trying. You're too heavy, I can't—" Ryan felt his father's wrist slip from his grasp. He couldn't do it. He couldn't hold on any longer.

"Why are you letting go?"

"I'm not!" Ryan yelled. But his dad suddenly fell away, screaming as his arms flailed and he dropped into the black chasm.

"Dad!"

Ryan's eyes snapped open. It took a few moments for him to realize it was all a nightmare. After a couple of deep breaths, he calmed down.

He'd been having dreams like this since he got back from Andakar. Being forced to leave his father behind while he continued the mission had been the hardest decision Ryan had ever made. He still felt guilty about it.

At first, he thought everything had worked out fine. Ryan finished the job his dad started, getting the rebel blogger Lan out of the hostile country and into the United States. The ERC found an older couple with no kids who took her in, and Lan traded the dangerous life of a spy for a new identity in the safety and comfort of Washington, DC. Chatting with her through an anonymous server a few days ago, Ryan was thrilled when Lan told him how much she loved it there.

Dad made it out of Andakar with the help of Tasha Levi, the tough and irritable operative who had first told Ryan about his family's involvement with the ERC. It had taken Tasha and Ryan's father three days to make it back to New York. But when they arrived, Ryan was shocked to see Dad's condition.

He was weak, barely able to move without help. Even worse, Dad couldn't remember anything from the past several days. It was like his brain was scrambled. The strangest part of all was that he now had no memory of the whole Andakar experience.

Ryan couldn't help but feel it was partially his fault—he wouldn't have left his dad if he'd known he was in such bad shape. They were just lucky Tasha found his dad's hiding place in the ancient temple and got him back home. If something awful had happened, Ryan would have never forgiven himself.

After one of his nightmares, getting back to sleep was almost impossible. Ryan's mind was racing in a million directions. There'd been so much to take in over the last few weeks.

Ryan quietly opened his door and shuffled into the hallway. He was about to go into the bathroom to get a glass of water when he heard something.

Voices, from downstairs. It was after midnight, and that didn't sound like his dad talking. Had someone broken in? Ryan moved to the stairway that connected all the floors of their home and listened.

But then he heard his mom. He'd recognize her French accent anywhere. She sounded worried. Ryan suspected it had something to do with whatever was going on with the ERC. He had to get closer.

The old brownstone where Ryan's family lived had belonged to his grandparents. Ryan loved the place, full of dark wood, high windows and history, but it was difficult to walk around without making noise. He moved slowly, navigating around the stairs that creaked the loudest.

Closer now, Ryan could make out at least four people talking. They were down on the basement level. His grandfather Declan had built a huge study down there, complete with a hidden room where all the ERC's secret files were kept. Last week, Ryan had wanted to read some of the files only to discover his dad had installed a new lock. Which didn't make a lot of sense because Dad had taught him how to pick locks when he was seven years old! Ryan was sorely tempted to break in and read the files anyway. So far, he had resisted the temptation, hoping his parents would soon trust him enough to share everything without him going behind their backs.

As Ryan made his way down the last set of stairs to the basement, the voices became more distinct.

". . . it can't be a coincidence." That was Dad talking. "Not two in one week."

A woman's voice responded. "The two incidents might be completely unrelated."

"None of us believe that," Mom said.

Ryan made it to the bottom stair. He could see the door into the study, the flickering light from a fire casting shadows around the room. But he couldn't see the people talking.

"I also heard earlier today that Salim Shah didn't show up for work this morning," Dad said. "No answer at his home. We can't confirm he's missing yet, but it seems likely."

"And no calls were made to the emergency number?" the woman asked.

"The emergency number has been disconnected. We didn't realize it until today, and I have no idea how it happened. It may take a few days to get it working again."

"It seems obvious that the ERC has been compromised." This was the other man in the room. From his accent, Ryan thought he might be Indian or Pakistani. "We must have a leak."

"We agree," Mom said. "That's why we wanted you here. We have no idea how they got their information, but—"

"Sneaky." Ryan whipped around in surprise at the whispered voice in his ear—Tasha Levi was right behind him. Tough and temperamental, Tasha was one of the ERC's best operatives. Somehow, she'd snuck up on him without making a sound. And now he was totally busted.

Tasha considered him a moment, then stepped around. "Lucky for you, I like sneaky."

Ryan took a chance. "I heard them say there's a leak. Who do you think it is?"

"Your parents don't want you involved."

"Maybe I can help."

Tasha didn't hide her amusement. "I think we can handle it. Nighty night."

Ryan glanced at the door one last time. Inside, the planning continued. Frustrated, he headed back upstairs. He didn't understand what was going on, but at least Tasha hadn't ratted him out.

At the top, he turned back. In the darkness, Tasha stared up at him. She didn't look amused anymore.

In fact, she looked pissed off.

CHAPTER
04

**NEW YORK,
USA**

S he's so into you, dude." Danny slammed his locker shut and faced Ryan. "You should call and ask her out."

Ryan rolled his eyes as they walked down the hallway. "Tasha's, like, twenty years old."

"Come on, she whispered in your ear." He mimicked Tasha's voice, giving it a ridiculous flirting quality, "'Lucky for you, I *like* sneaky.'"

Ryan laughed. "She'd strangle you if she heard you do that."

"Nah, I'd distract her with my charm. She wouldn't stand a chance." Danny's expression suddenly changed. "So what do you think happened to those people your parents said are missing?"

"I don't know."

"Get me the names. Maybe I can uncover something online that will help find them." Danny was an incredible hacker. He could access websites and databases that were strictly off-limits to civilians. He was always careful to cover his tracks, but Ryan was afraid that someday his friend would get into serious trouble. If these people were in danger, though, maybe it was worth the risk?

"I'll see what I can find out," Ryan said.

"This is exactly what we need. A way to prove to your parents that they should be making us part of the team." Danny stopped in front of a classroom door. "All right, last exam for the semester. Next time I see you, we will officially be unshackled and on winter break!"

Ryan hurried to his English class. They'd just finished studying T. H. White's *The Once and Future King*, and most of the final was supposed to be an essay on King Arthur. Ryan had loved the first part of the book where the wizard Merlyn changed young Arthur into lots of different animals—that sounded like a blast. But the last sections were pretty depressing. Arthur lost everything and was even betrayed by his family. He learned too late the lesson that Merlyn tried to teach him as a boy: A good leader understands that having power doesn't necessarily make him right.

The kids in Ryan's English class had plenty to say about that. There had been a lot of lively discussions. That's what was so great about the International Community School of New York. Most of the students were the children of people who worked at the nearby United Nations Headquarters. They came from all over the world, and a lot of them had lived at least part of their lives in troubled countries.

As he turned the corner, Ryan stopped in surprise. His mom was standing outside the classroom, talking to Principal Milankovic. What was *she* doing here? Was he in some kind of trouble? As he got closer, Ryan could see they were arguing. Milankovic was a bear of a man; he towered over Jacqueline. But whatever they were discussing, she didn't back down. She shook her head and held her ground.

Ryan wondered if the disagreement had to do with the odd comment Principal Milankovic made to him at the dance last month. "But you deserve the truth," the principal had told him. "The truth about who you really are." What did that even mean? And how could the principal know stuff about him since Ryan had only been going to school here a few months?

When he saw him at school a few days later, Ryan asked Milankovic about it. The principal had been uncomfortable, mumbling that he had confused Ryan with another student. It was obvious he was lying, especially since he'd gone out of his way to avoid Ryan since then.

As Ryan approached, Milankovic saw him and cut off whatever he was about to say. He was definitely angry. Jacqueline turned, and Ryan noticed that she had his duffel bag slung over one shoulder.

"What's going on?"

"I'm sorry to just show up like this. I know you have a test."

"Which starts in less than a minute," Principal Milankovic said, checking a pocket watch he carried. "Make this quick, please."

He nodded curtly to Jaqcueline, then walked off.

"Were you guys arguing?" Ryan asked.

"Listen, I know this is short notice," Mom said, dodging the question. "But Dad and I have to go to Chicago tonight."

"Something else happened, didn't it?" Ryan whispered. The last of his classmates passed into the room as the sixth-period bell rang. "Is someone else missing?"

Mom's eyes narrowed. "How do you know about that?"

"I'd know a lot more if you'd just trust me."

"No, you need to trust *us*. You may not understand our reasons, but we're doing what we think is best." The worry showed in her expression as she handed him the duffel bag. "We'll talk more when we're home, but we have to go check this out ourselves, okay?"

Ryan put the bag on his shoulder. "How long will you be gone?"

"Hopefully, just overnight. I called Danny's mom and told her Dad had a last-minute work conference this weekend. You can stay with them. I packed everything I thought you might need. You should go. Your test is starting."

"Take me with you."

"Not this time." Mom leaned in and kissed his cheek. "I'll text you once we're there. We'll be back before you know it. I love you."

She took a few steps away before he called out, "Mom!" Jacqueline turned back. "I love you, too."

That brought a smile. She blew him another

kiss. "Good luck on your test! Go, before you get in trouble!"

Then she was gone. Reluctantly, Ryan headed into the classroom. But King Arthur was the last thing on his mind now.

CHAPTER
05

**NEW YORK,
USA**

T his is a bad idea." Kasey glanced around like they were doing something illegal as Ryan unlocked the front door of the brownstone. It was still late afternoon, but the sun was already setting, evening coming early during the winter months.

"It's *his* house," Danny said. "He's got a key."

"So you're not planning to go down to the study and snoop into all the ERC files?" Kasey looked between them, but neither boy met her accusatory gaze. "That's what I thought."

Ryan opened the door, and they stepped inside. "We just want to help."

"If we can find the names of whoever's missing," Danny said, "there's a chance I can track down something online that'll help locate them."

Kasey wasn't convinced. "I want to be a part of everything just as much as you guys. But this doesn't feel right."

Kasey had a point. Ryan considered leaving now and just waiting for his parents to get back from Chicago. But he'd seen how worried Mom and Dad were. If there was even a chance of helping, shouldn't they at least try?

Ryan turned to Danny. "Are you sure you can do these searches without anybody else knowing?"

"Positive," Danny said. "I'll create a virtual machine and use an encrypted private tunnel. Plus, I'll make sure I only backdoor the databases using a botnet and some web filters."

Ryan glanced at Kasey, who shrugged, then back to Danny. "I've got no idea what you said, but it sounds good. Come on."

Ryan led them downstairs. With no fire burning, the study felt cold and uninviting. Flipping on a light, he headed to the far end of the room. The rear wall appeared to be made of solid brick. In reality, the whole wall was a large door that concealed the secret room where the ERC files and equipment were hidden. Ryan removed the fake bricks that masked the door's handle.

Danny came up behind him. "Can you pick it?"

The lock Ryan's dad had installed was a newer brand, designed to be resistant to lock-picks. But Ryan wasn't worried. "Give me three minutes," he said.

Ryan's key ring held the brownstone keys and a strangely shaped metallic object his dad had given him on his twelfth birthday. A multi-purpose tool, it could be used as a screwdriver, bottle opener, wire cutter, or tweezers. Hidden inside were thin strips of metal. One was a tension wrench, the other a lockpick with a hook at the end. Not what every kid got for their birthday, but it had been perfect for Ryan. With a delicate touch, he inserted the picks into the lock's tumbler and got to work.

"Maybe if you jiggled it a little more . . . ?" Danny said.

Ryan didn't look back. "Not helping."

Danny reluctantly walked away, giving him room to work. The trick to picking was visualizing what was happening inside the lock, seeing the pins in your mind as they set into position. Ryan closed his eyes, concentrating only on what he felt with his fingertips. One by one, the pins clicked into place.

"You were a cute kid," Kasey said. Ryan opened his eyes and glanced back. Kasey stood at the bookshelves, a photo album open in her hands.

"Kinda chubby," Danny pointed out, looking over her shoulder.

"Just his tummy." She smiled at Ryan. "You had a Winnie-the-Pooh tummy. Very cute."

"Adorable," Danny teased.

Click. Ryan felt the last pin set into position, and the lock sprung open. "I'm in," he said, thankful for the distraction. He opened the door, revealing the small room beyond, as Danny joined him. "There are some files on the table. Maybe those are the people that are missing."

Kasey came toward them, flipping the pages of the photo album. "Where are the baby pictures?"

"I thought you were looking at them."

"I mean like when you were first born. You're already about a year old in these."

"Those are all of them, as far as I know." Actually, Ryan hadn't looked at the album in a long time. His family used to move so often that it was mostly kept stored in a box. Now that they were living here permanently, Mom was finally able to have it out. He glanced at the photo, embarrassed—Kasey was right, he *did* have a chubby tummy!

Ryan snapped the album shut, setting it aside. "No more baby pictures."

"Hey," Danny interrupted. "Your parents went to Chicago, right?"

"Yeah."

"None of these files have actual names on them—everybody's referred to by codes and stuff. But look at this." Danny handed Ryan an article that had been cut from the newspaper. The headline read: "Local Teacher Missing, Police Request Public's Help." "This is from Chicago. It must be why they went there."

Ryan nodded, when a loud thud from upstairs made them all jump.

Danny looked at the ceiling. "You don't have a new cat we don't know about, do you?"

Ryan shook his head. That was no cat.

Somebody was in the house.

CHAPTER
06

**NEW YORK,
USA**

R yan grabbed a log from the wood stacked next to the fireplace. It wasn't a great weapon, but it would have to do.

"Stay here," he told Kasey and Danny.

"Uh-uh," Kasey said.

"No way." Danny grabbed a log and handed it to Kasey, then took one for himself. "Three's better than one."

Ryan could tell arguing wouldn't help. "Okay, but if we see a gun, everybody run."

"Sounds like excellent advice," Danny whispered.

Together, the trio crept back up the stairs. The sun had set, plunging the brownstone into deep shadows. Near the top, Ryan paused, listening. He could hear someone moving quietly in the rear of the house. They must have broken into the kitchen from the back garden.

Ryan crossed the living room quickly, hoping to get to the light switch on the far wall before the intruder entered. With the element of surprise on his side, Ryan might be able to disarm the thief.

He was almost to the switch when the wooden stair behind him creaked. Ryan spun around as Danny froze. But it was too late. There was no more movement from the kitchen. The intruder had heard the noise and would now be ready for them.

Ryan didn't waste a second. He raised the log with one hand and stepped into the kitchen, turning on the lights.

"Yaaahhh!!" he yelled, trying to sound intimidating. Behind him, Danny and Kasey raced forward, also yelling like they were crazed Vikings.

The intruder screamed in terror! He stumbled backward, falling over one of the kitchen chairs and landing hard. He raised his hands and ducked his head as the three kids surrounded him.

Feeling empowered, Danny stepped forward.

"We got him! Call the cops!"

As the man glanced up, though, Ryan saw confusion and fear in his eyes. He was in his early twenties and black, dressed in a gray suit and blue tie. Ryan thought he looked more like a young accountant than a thief. Kasey lowered her log, sensing he wasn't really a threat. "Who are you?" she asked.

"The emergency number was disconnected," the man said. "I didn't know where else to go."

Ryan set his log on the table, then looked to Danny. "I don't think we need these." He approached the young man, noticing now that his business suit was dirty and the knees were stained, probably from climbing over the back wall into the garden. "My name is Ryan. This is my house you broke into."

"Wait, this isn't Declan Quinn's home?"

"It was. Declan was my grandfather."

"Where is he?" he asked urgently. His English was accented; Ryan guessed it wasn't his first language. "I have to speak with him."

"I'm sorry. Declan died last year. My family lives here now." Ryan felt Danny move up behind him. "But maybe I can help. What's your name?"

"Lawrence Cain." Ryan stood and held out a hand, helping him up. "I didn't break in. There was a key hidden in the garden. Mr. Quinn said to use it if we ever needed to. I had to be careful no one saw me."

He held out the key, returning it. Ryan hadn't known about a hidden key, and he didn't think his parents did, either. But it seemed like Lawrence was telling the truth.

Kasey stepped forward. "Are you involved with the Emergency Rescue Committee?"

Lawrence looked at the three of them, surprised. "You know about the ERC?"

"Oh yeah. We're all a part of it," Danny said. "Practically."

"We know there's been trouble recently." Ryan didn't completely trust this guy yet. His parents and the other ERC members said the group might be compromised, so he had to be cautious. But maybe he could find out something useful if he got Lawrence to talk. "You said you called the emergency number. Why'd you do that?"

Ryan was surprised to see Lawrence's eyes suddenly moisten. The young man was overwhelmed.

"Someone's taken her," he said. "I came home, and she was gone. They've taken Nadia."

CHAPTER 07

NEW YORK, USA

Seated in the brownstone's living room, Lawrence explained that he and Nadia had been sentenced to death in their home country of Lovanda in central Africa. They would have been executed if not for Declan Quinn and the ERC. With help from a group of locals, Declan and his associates orchestrated a jailbreak and managed to smuggle Lawrence and Nadia out of Lovanda and onto an ocean freighter that eventually brought them to America.

"Wait a minute," Ryan interrupted. "How old were you when this happened?"

"It was five years ago. I was barely eighteen."

Kasey couldn't believe it, either. "You were

teenagers and sentenced to death? What did you do?"

"We made the wrong people mad," Lawrence said. He was a bundle of nerves, biting his thumbnail as his knee bounced involuntarily. "We were young and stupid. Thought we were invincible."

"Did you kill someone?" Danny asked.

"No. We made music." Lawrence looked away, lost in some distant memory. "We were just kids. We thought we could change the world with our songs. But some things can't be changed."

Before coming into the living room, Danny had retrieved his computer from downstairs. His fingers flew over the keys. He spun the laptop around so they could all see. "Anbo and Delilah— this is you?"

Lawrence barely glanced at the monitor. "Not anymore."

"This video's got over a million hits," Danny said, hitting play. "You two were popular."

It was a concert video recorded with a cell phone. The sound quality wasn't great, but Ryan could still feel the rage behind the performance. A rapper wearing long dreadlocks and a tie-dyed T-shirt captivated the crowd. Pacing the small stage with furious energy, he rapped of growing up so poor that he had to dig through trash to find things to sell to support his family.

Ryan looked from the video to the restless young man with the close-cropped hair in disbelief. This guy radiated anxiety, like he was gonna jump out of his skin at any moment. But Ryan recognized the high forehead and deep-set eyes shared by the rapper in the video. The man sitting next to them was the same passionate firebrand who had performed on a stage for a cheering audience.

Kasey obviously felt the same. "You were a rapper?"

"I was a poet, but nobody cared. When I put my words to a beat, to music, they started listening." In the video, the crowd roared its approval. A woman's voice, commanding and haunting, suddenly rose above the noise. The cell phone video jiggled around and found the singer onstage. Lawrence appeared pained as he confirmed, "That's her. That's Delilah."

Delilah—or Nadia, as she was now known—was tall and striking. She wore flowing robes of gold and white. The crowd hushed as she sang about rising up against the corruption that surrounded them.

"Enough." Lawrence leaned forward and hit

the space bar, stopping the video. "This foolishness cost us everything before. And now they've found us again."

"Who? Who took her?" Ryan asked.

Lawrence rubbed his eyes as he told them how he was coming home from his job as a bank teller when he noticed a strange man watching their apartment. The man was concealed in the shadows, but Lawrence managed to duck out of sight before he got spotted. He snuck around back and entered their apartment. Inside, he realized that he was already too late. There was an overturned table and chair, but Nadia was gone.

"She was recording songs," Lawrence finished. "That could be how they tracked us down. If she put the songs online, someone might have recognized her voice. I warned her not to."

"I don't think it's Nadia's fault," Ryan assured him. "Other people the ERC saved have also gone missing. Somehow, their new identities are being discovered."

Danny's phone buzzed and he glanced down, reading a text. "It's my mom. We're supposed to be at my place already."

Kasey stood up. "I have to get home, too."

Ryan looked to Lawrence. "You can stay here

tonight. My mom and dad are in Chicago, but I'll call and tell them what's going on. They'll know what to do."

"And we'll help them," Danny said, stuffing his laptop in his backpack. "We'll find Nadia."

But Lawrence still seemed defeated. "You don't know these people. We embarrassed them when we disappeared. They'll never forget that. They won't stop until we're both dead."

Ryan put a hand on his shoulder. "I promise you, we'll do everything we can to help."

"I just hope it's not already too late."

Ryan wished there was something more encouraging he could say. But in his heart, he worried Lawrence was right.

CHAPTER
08

**NEW YORK,
USA**

anny's home was always filled with noise. His sisters, Analyn and Lilibeth, were four-year-old twins who couldn't be more different. Analyn was into the whole princess thing and pressed Ryan into duty as Prince Charming in her elaborate make-believe adventures. Lilibeth was sportier, kicking a soccer ball around the apartment or begging Ryan to play catch with her. A typical big brother, Danny couldn't be bothered with the girls' games, so they clung to Ryan whenever he visited.

The Santiagos lived in a three-bedroom apartment on the sixth floor of an older building. The rooms were small and jam-packed with furniture and knickknacks. With either music or the television playing at all times, there was never a dull moment.

Ryan loved it.

Growing up an only child, he had often imagined what it would be like to come from a big family. He got along great with his mom and dad, but it was sometimes quiet with just the three of them. Plus, one or the other was often traveling, which left only two. Being around Danny's boisterous, close-knit family made him realize how different life might have been.

"Dinner!" Mrs. Santiago shouted from the kitchen.

"We're not done!" Analyn yelled back, spinning around so her princess costume flared out. "Ryan still has to slay the dragon!"

"*I'm* gonna do the slaying if you don't wash your hands and sit at that table in one minute!"

Analyn turned to Ryan, who held a sword made from an old paper towel roll. "Can we finish after dinner?"

"Sure," Ryan said. "But next time, you have to be the dragon."

"I love being the dragon!" Analyn hurried off as Danny entered the living room.

"You don't have to play with her," he said.

"Just tell her to get lost."

"It's fun." Ryan lunged forward and stabbed the pretend sword into Danny's stomach. "Got ya!"

Danny grinned. "Careful. In your hands, that thing's probably a lethal weapon."

Ryan called out to Analyn. "It's safe to come out, Princess Starbright. I killed the grumpy dragon with the wild hair!"

"Hysterical," Danny said.

As they approached the dinner table, he whispered to Ryan. "I've been doing some digging into everything Lawrence told us. I think I found some really good leads we can check out tomorrow."

"We can't do anything until we hear from Mom or Dad." Ryan had spoken briefly to his father about meeting Lawrence and told him that Nadia had been taken. Dad was in a rush and couldn't talk, but promised they'd figure out what to do and call back as soon as possible.

Danny was impatient, though. "But wait'll you hear what all I found—"

"Sit, Ryan," Mrs. Santiago said, coming out of the kitchen with a steaming dish. "Daniel, get the *pinakbet*—it's on the counter."

"Got it." Danny disappeared into the kitchen.

Mrs. Santiago placed the dish on the table. "I hope you like adobo."

"I love it," Ryan assured her, breathing in the wonderful aroma of the garlic-and-soy-sauce-flavored pork dish, a Filipino staple. The twins and Mr. Santiago, a cheerful man with a booming voice, joined them. Everyone talked at once as they took their seats.

The food was delicious. It was the kind of normal family dinner Ryan usually enjoyed at Danny's house. But his mind was elsewhere: worried about his parents in Chicago; unsure how to help Lawrence and Nadia; curious to hear the information Danny had uncovered.

When Mr. Santiago asked why his parents were away, Ryan told him the cover story Mom gave him about a last-minute work conference. The lie came easily, almost without even thinking about it. He hated being dishonest, but it was necessary to protect the ERC.

After dinner, Ryan and Danny cleaned up and did the dishes. As soon as they were done, the boys retreated to Danny's room and closed the door. Finally having privacy, Danny updated Ryan on what he'd found.

"Anbo and Delilah were a big deal before they got arrested. Their other songs are like the one we heard. Superpolitical, all about what's wrong with their country."

"We learned about Lovanda when I lived in Africa," Ryan said. "It was a British colony for a long time, right?"

"Yeah. And then there was this civil war that went on for years. Now it's supposedly a democracy, but the same party's been in power for over twenty years. The government controls everything—TV, music, the internet. Anybody who speaks out against them gets thrown in jail or executed."

"So Anbo and Delilah knew how dangerous it was performing those songs."

"That's why they could only do pop-up concerts. No warning. They'd just get up wherever they could and start rapping these intense revolutionary songs. People loved them. The concerts were getting bigger and bigger."

Ryan could tell Danny was captivated by the idea. "I bet the government didn't like that."

"No," Danny agreed. "But there was one woman in particular who was seriously pissed."

Danny brought up a photo of an African woman. Her braided hair was pulled back, and she wore blue designer eyeglasses, pearl earrings, and a luxurious gown. Ryan thought her smile seemed really fake.

"Evelyn Buku," Danny said. "But every-one calls her Madame Buku. She's the richest woman in Lovanda. She owns a company called Sekhmet Technologies. The government in Lovanda is actually pretty poor. The real power is in the hands of a few business owners—and Madame Buku is the most powerful of them all."

"Lawrence said they made the wrong people mad," Ryan recalled.

"Yeah, they wrote songs about her. Called her the evil stepmother, like in *Cinderella*."

"You think she's responsible for taking Nadia?"

Danny nodded. "From everything I read, she's the one who got them arrested. She had her own private security force go after them, then bribed the judges to make sure they got the death penalty. She was furious when they escaped."

Ryan followed his logic. "She must have heard one of the songs Nadia released and redoubled her efforts to find them. If this woman's that rich, she could afford to track Lawrence and Nadia down if she really wanted to."

"Exactly! She even said in a few interviews that she's determined to see Anbo and Delilah returned to Lovanda to pay for their crimes."

"So if we could somehow figure out who sold her the information, we might also figure out who the leak inside the ERC is, right?"

"Maybe so." Danny perked up. "Hey, you said 'we.' As in you and me, working as a team? Doing the whole Batman and Robin thing?"

"We're not Batman and Robin," Ryan said.

"Lone Ranger and Tonto?"

Ryan shook his head and smiled. "So what else do we know about this Madame Buku?"

CHAPTER
09

**NEW YORK,
USA**

The next morning, Ryan woke to the buzz of his cell phone. He grabbed it, but the Caller ID read "Blocked."

"Hello?"

"Hey, bud. It's Dad."

"What's this number?" Ryan asked, sitting up in his sleeping bag and rubbing his eyes.

"We're not sure how safe our communications are. Mom and I picked up a couple of burner phones." His father sounded strained and tired. "The police found the man we were searching for. He'd been killed."

"Oh my god," Ryan said, as Danny turned over in his bed and opened his eyes. "Do they know who did it?"

"They don't have a clue. Unfortunately, there's not much more we can do here. We'll fly back today. We should be home by early afternoon."

"But we need to find Nadia. Tonight could be too late."

Danny threw back the comforter, swinging his legs around. "Tell them about Madame Buku and her plane."

"Dad, Danny and I have some ideas—"

"We already talked to Tasha," Dad interrupted. "She'll get Lawrence somewhere safe, then look for Nadia."

"What about us? We can help."

"Ryan, a man was *killed* here last night. You and your friends have to stay out of this. What were you doing at the brownstone last night, anyway?"

Ryan hesitated. "Just forgot a book I needed for school."

"You're out on winter break." Ryan could have kicked himself. Clearly, he wasn't nearly as good at lying to his parents as they were at lying to him. "We can talk about it when we get home. Just lay low until then, okay?"

"Yeah, I got it." They said good-bye, and Ryan ended the call, frustrated.

Danny could tell they were being shut out

again. "So what are we supposed to do? Just sit here and act like everything's fine?"

"That's what they want us to do."

"But what about Madame Buku's private jet? You didn't even get to tell them about that." Last night, Danny had found an online registration for a Boeing 727 that Madame Buku used for her travels around the world. Tracking the tail numbers that identified the plane, Danny discovered its current flight plan on the FAA's public database. Right now, the jet was parked at Fairfax Executive Airport, a private airfield in New Jersey, less than an hour from Manhattan. That couldn't be a coincidence.

"Dad said Tasha's gonna help Lawrence. I'll call and we can tell her what we found." Ryan didn't use Tasha's real name in his contacts list just in case he ever lost his phone, but he'd given her an alias that was easy to remember: Miss Crabby.

As Ryan dialed, Danny hopped out of bed and threw on a T-shirt and jeans. "Just make sure she knows the information came from us. We have to get full credit so they take us seriously next time."

The call went straight to voice mail. Remembering his father's fear that the phones might be tapped, Ryan kept his message vague. "Hey, it's Ryan and Danny. Call us back as soon as you can. It's important." He disconnected, then looked to Danny. "You know, she could be over at my house right now getting him."

"Then what are we doing *here*?" Danny grabbed Ryan's clothes and tossed them at him. "Let's go."

Five minutes later they were headed out, but Mrs. Santiago intercepted them at the door, insisting they have breakfast. Danny promised his mom they'd stop for a bagel but said they had to hurry to the basketball courts at Chelsea Piers for a pickup game with friends.

"Basketball? Instead of sitting in front of a computer screen all day?" She couldn't have been more thrilled and turned to Ryan, smiling. "You're such a good influence!"

"Bye, *nanay*!" Danny hustled out, assuring his mom they'd check in later.

As the door closed behind them, Ryan turned to Danny, impressed. "How do you do that? My parents always catch me when I lie to them."

Danny shrugged. "Just tell them what they want to hear. Works every time."

It was ten blocks from Danny's building to

Ryan's brownstone. They ran the whole way. By the time they turned the corner onto 62nd Street, Danny was winded and wheezing. The boys suddenly stopped dead in their tracks.

Up ahead, a police car was parked in the middle of the street, lights flashing. A few people were gathered at the curb in front of the Quinns' brownstone talking with a uniformed cop.

"Lawrence," Ryan muttered, then started forward.

Danny grabbed his arm. "Wait. If you go up there, they're gonna ask you all kinds of questions. Questions you might not want to answer."

"We have to find out what happened."

"I know. But let me go check first and see what's going on. Nobody on this block knows me."

Ryan agreed, seeing Danny's point. "I'll try Tasha again."

Danny attempted to look casual, making his way across the street to the people gathered on the sidewalk.

Ryan took out his phone and dialed. If the same people who took Nadia had Lawrence now, there wasn't much time. They'd either be dead or taken back to Lovanda quickly.

"What?" Tasha's brusque answer caught Ryan off guard.

"Hey—I left a message for you earlier."

"I've been busy. What do you want?" Tasha's impatience irritated Ryan.

"Do you have Lawrence?" Ryan glanced at the brownstone as a second officer came out the front door.

"No. I went to your house after your parents called. But it looked like somebody got there before me. He was gone."

Ryan was angry at himself. "I should've never left him alone."

"Then you'd be missing, too. Or worse." Tasha's tone softened. "I'm doing everything I can to find him."

"That's why I called earlier. There's this woman, she really hates them—and she's super-rich. Danny and I think she may be the one who's after Lawrence and Nadia."

"She's here in New York?"

"I don't know, but—"

"Then how is that going to help me find them?" Tasha spat. "We're wasting time."

Ryan barely stopped himself from snapping back at her. "I'm not sure if *she's* in New York, but her private jet *is*. Or it's close anyway—the flight plan they logged says it arrived at Fair-fax Executive Airport two days ago. That's just across the river, in Englewood. And they're scheduled to leave later today."

Tasha was quiet a moment, considering. "Okay, I'll check it out."

"Danny and I can meet you there."

"You'll only slow me down. I can't do my job and look out for two kids at the same time."

"I did fine before."

"I'll text you if I find anything." The call disconnected. Ryan was sick of being dismissed by the adults in his life.

Danny hurried back across the street, eager to share what he'd learned. "Your neighbor called the cops. She was picking up her newspaper and saw the front door standing open. The lock was shattered, like someone broke in."

"Tasha said she came to get Lawrence, but they'd already been here."

Danny looked back at the two uniformed cops. "They're trying to get in touch with your parents now. What should we do?"

Ryan considered his options, then suddenly stepped off the curb and into the street. "Taxi!"

A passing yellow cab pulled over, screeching to a stop. Ryan opened the back door and turned to Danny. "I'm going to Fairfax Executive Airport."

"Not by yourself, you're not!" Danny scurried past Ryan into the backseat. Ryan followed him in and slammed the door.

No more sitting on the sidelines.

It was time to get in the game.

CHAPTER
10

**NEW JERSEY,
USA**

The kid was turning into a problem.

Tasha kept her eyes on the road, but her thoughts were focused on Ryan Quinn. He and his computer-geek friend were stubborn and independent. But they were also naive. They reminded her a little of herself at that age.

Though she definitely wasn't naive anymore.

Tasha glanced in the backseat of her BMW. Lawrence Cain was still unconscious, hands bound and mouth gagged.

This kind of thing wasn't part of her agreement with Braxton Crisp. She was furious that he'd forced her to do it. Like she was some common thug. But it wasn't smart to cross Crisp. He might not look intimidating in his tweed jacket and ridiculous bow ties, but Crisp was vicious. She'd once seen him shove a man off a rooftop to his death without giving it a second thought.

How the hell did she end up doing his dirty work?

It was her own fault.

She should have told him no when he first approached her. But Tasha was still grieving the death of her father. Her dad had been Tasha's whole world. He'd raised her single-handedly since her mother left them both when she was eleven. Isaac Levi had been a soldier most of his life and brought his daughter up to be tough and resourceful—just like him.

When Tasha learned of Isaac's secret work with the Emergency Rescue Committee, she begged him to let her help. To her surprise, he readily agreed. Isaac trained her to be an operative, and by the time she was sixteen, Tasha was going on missions around the world. She loved every minute of it.

Until the day Isaac didn't come home.

When John Quinn showed up at her door, she knew instantly that her father was dead. John explained that he and Isaac had been in Iran, attempting to help a scientist and his family get out of the country. Things went wrong, and Isaac tried to buy them time to escape. Quinn got the family to safety, but Isaac didn't make it out. He died a hero.

Tasha was crushed. She didn't want a hero. She wanted her father back.

For over a year after her father's death, Tasha channeled her anger and pain into her work for the ERC. She'd help anyone anywhere who needed her.

But four months ago, Braxton Crisp changed all that. He told her he had proof that John Quinn lied. Her father had been abandoned and left to die by the ERC. The truth was that John Quinn had betrayed Isaac, valuing his own safety over her father's life.

Of course, she didn't believe him at first. But Crisp played a recording of Quinn on his cell phone. She heard her father's closest friend say that Isaac had been wounded. Quinn insisted it was too risky to go back. Isaac's injuries were severe enough that he probably wouldn't survive anyway.

Tasha was in shock. The first rule of the ERC is that you never leave a man behind. The work was too dangerous—they had to be able to trust each other with their lives. Crisp was right: John

Quinn *had* abandoned her father. He left Isaac to die, all alone.

Crisp told her he had a way for her to get vengeance for her father's death. A scheme that would expose John Quinn and destroy the ERC forever.

And would also make them both very rich in the process.

They strategized for weeks and were finally able to put their plan into action in Andakar. When Quinn had been shot helping Lan escape, it provided Tasha the perfect opportunity. Taking advantage of his weakened state, she had no trouble surprising Quinn and knocking him out. She delivered him to Crisp, who gave John a powerful truth serum. Quinn couldn't help himself—he told Crisp about every ERC rescue he remembered, divulging the confidential new identities and locations of over thirty people.

After Crisp got all the information he needed from John Quinn, Tasha flew him back home. By design, Quinn had no memory of the entire three days. He went back to his normal life with no clue that he had just given up the entire ERC organization.

In the backseat, Lawrence moaned.

Crisp sold the location of Lawrence and

Nadia for almost two million dollars. Tasha's cut had been more money than she'd possessed in her whole life. But the windfall came at a cost. Crisp now acted like she worked for him, ordering her to do things she'd never agreed to.

Tasha saw the sign for the rest area where she was supposed to drop off Lawrence. She pulled around back, determined to get rid of him as fast as possible.

Tasha had maintained her cover for months and didn't plan on blowing it now. She hoped Ryan and his friends didn't get too nosy. Tasha really didn't want to hurt them.

But if necessary, she would.

CHAPTER

11

**NEW JERSEY,
USA**

We're here." Ryan glanced at Danny as the taxi pulled into the parking lot of the Fairfax Executive Airport. Danny's thumbs flew over the keys of his phone. "What're you doing?"

"Hacking the tracking software on my phone." He looked up as the taxi came to a stop. "Done. Now, if my mom checks on us, it'll look like we're at Chelsea Piers."

"You know, you'd make an awesome evil genius," Ryan said.

"True. But I prefer to use my powers for good."

Ryan paid the cabdriver and they got out. The tiny but exclusive airfield was in the middle of nowhere, surrounded by a chain-link fence. A single building housed the terminal and a flight tower. The runway was flanked by several rows of long, white hangars that sheltered private air-craft.

"That's it," Danny said, pointing.

A large plane stood at the end of the runway. Ryan had flown on countless trips growing up, so he instantly recognized it as an older 727. It had probably once been a commercial passenger plane, but was now converted into a luxurious VIP jet. The tail fin displayed the stylized head of a lion, the logo of Sekhmet Technologies.

"We need to get closer." Ryan kept himself hidden behind parked cars as he maneuvered along the fence. There wasn't much security at this airfield, which might be why Madame Buku used it.

Danny crept along behind Ryan. "What do we do if Lawrence and Nadia are really in there?"

"Tasha should be here somewhere. Maybe she's got a plan."

Using a van for cover, Ryan peered out at Madame Buku's jet. Members of the crew swarmed around, preparing for takeoff. Two sets of stairs were open, one close to the front for passengers and another at the rear where food and supplies were being loaded.

"I don't see them." Ryan studied the fence. It was about eight feet high, but didn't have any barbed wire on top. "Stay here."

Ryan moved to the front of the parked van. He checked to make sure no one was watching, then jumped onto the hood.

"What are you doing?" Danny said.

"Getting a better view." Ryan hopped to the van's roof. He sprinted toward the fence, then leaped. Ryan's hands hit the top of the fence, and he catapulted over. He sailed through the air and landed hard on the asphalt below, cushioning the impact by dropping into a roll.

Ryan got back to his feet and scurried behind a parked twin-engine Beechcraft for cover. He glanced back through the chain link at his friend. Danny gave him a thumbs-up.

About thirty yards to his right, Ryan spotted an orange fuel tank truck. Keeping low, he ran toward it. He leaned against the tanker and peered around the rear. The captain and copilot were now climbing the front stairs to board the jet, but there was no sign of Lawrence or Nadia.

Maybe he and Danny were wrong. Maybe this woman wasn't responsible for taking them after all.

Ryan was trying to figure out what to do next when his phone buzzed. It was a text from Danny: *stay low. black SUVs incoming.*

Suddenly, a door slammed and the engine of the fuel truck roared to life! Ryan was on the passenger side and hadn't even seen the driver get in. The truck was moving and would leave Ryan exposed.

A metal ladder that provided access to the top of the tank was attached to the truck. Ryan grabbed the ladder, praying the driver didn't check his side mirror. As the truck drove toward the jet, he climbed up and pressed himself flat along the top.

The tank truck pulled to the far side of the jet and stopped once more. Ryan slid to the edge so the driver couldn't see him as he got out. The tanker rumbled as the equipment powered up.

Ryan watched as two black SUVs arrived and jerked to a stop in front of the passenger stairway. The doors of both SUVs opened and five rough-looking guys stepped out. A muscular man with a military cut and a nasty scar down the side of his face seemed to be in charge. Ryan couldn't hear over the noise of the tank truck, but the man was barking orders to the others.

The back door of the second SUV opened. Ryan had to risk inching forward so he could see. A young black woman stepped out looking scared but defiant. She appeared very different from the video, but Ryan instantly recognized her: It was Nadia. Struggling in the grip of her captor, she looked over as one of the men dragged Lawrence out.

Lawrence could barely stand. He looked like he'd been drugged, his head drooping to one side. Nadia snapped at the men, saying something Ryan couldn't hear. She was definitely a fighter. The scarred leader grabbed her arm and shoved her toward the stairway while another man half carried Lawrence behind them.

Ryan grabbed his phone, frantic. He had to stop them. Where was Tasha, and why wasn't she doing something?

He texted her: *are you at airport? is there a plan?*

Ryan slid off the tanker and dropped to the ground. He hoped Tasha had something in mind, because he had no idea how to stop these guys from leaving.

His phone buzzed. Ryan read Tasha's text in confusion.

already went to airport. they weren't there. sorry.

That didn't make any sense. If she'd been here, she must have seen the jet. It was the biggest plane on the runway.

Which meant she didn't really come to the airport.

Tasha was lying.

CHAPTER 12

**NEW JERSEY,
USA**

Having a friend like Ryan Quinn was incredible. But when your best friend can jump over eight-foot-high fences or knock out grown-ups with a well-placed martial arts kick, it was sometimes hard not to feel a little second-rate. Sure, Danny was great with technology, but he didn't think that was anywhere near as cool as what Ryan could do.

Not that he was complaining. Since Ryan arrived a few months ago, Danny's whole life was better. He could hang out with Ryan for hours, just talking and listening to music. Ryan even liked Danny's crazy family. Plus, he knew Ryan always had his back.

Danny just wished that sometimes he felt more like the hero and less like the sidekick.

Standing outside the fence of the private airfield, he knew immediately that the two SUVs that went inside were bad news. If Ryan got into trouble, there was nothing Danny could do from out here.

Danny couldn't leap over that fence like Ryan did. But maybe there was another way in. He jogged to the front door of the small terminal building and went inside. There wasn't much to it, just one large room. Upscale, with lots of wood and glass. A few people sat scattered in lounge chairs waiting for flights. At the far end was a counter where an attendant was helping customers. Sliding doors led to the tarmac and runway, but the lone security guard looked bored. He paid more attention to his book than to the handful of travelers milling about.

Danny's spiky hair and unconventional clothes always stood out in a crowd. He did it on purpose, having lived most of his life feeling almost invisible. But right now, being invisible was exactly what he wanted.

Danny ducked into the men's bathroom and

went to the sink. Quickly, he ran his hands under running water and wet his hair. He smoothed it down as much as possible, pressing it tight against his head. Not perfect, but better. He took off his bomber jacket, leaving only the hoodie and T-shirt he wore underneath. Just a normal teenager.

And who's more invisible to adults than a normal teenager?

Danny exited the men's room and headed for the runway doors. A group of four passengers was just gathering their things and heading out. They carried duffels and a long bag that looked like it held skis. Danny filed in right behind them, head bent over his phone as if he was texting and couldn't be bothered to look up.

"Let me get those for you, sir." A porter in a red jacket took the ski bag from the man in front of Danny. "The Learjet is just over here to the left, everyone."

Danny's heart was beating fast. The security guard glanced up as they all went out the door. Danny kept his head bowed, not daring to look up until he was safely out on the tarmac.

His group headed toward a sleek jet as Danny veered toward the much bigger 727. No one even noticed. Other red-jacketed porters unloaded bags from the SUVs and put them on the kind of rolling carts that bellboys use. This place was more like a fancy hotel than an airport.

As a cart rolled past, Danny fell into step beside it, using the luggage as a shield. He glanced up at the stairway that led into the jet just in time to see a man supporting Lawrence, practically dragging him into the plane. Lawrence stumbled and nearly fell. The man jerked him to his feet, and they disappeared inside.

Danny quickly texted Ryan, making sure he knew Lawrence was onboard the jet.

Danny's camouflage suddenly stopped moving. The porter left the cart and went back to get the rest of the bags. Danny was stranded at a conveyer belt used to transport the luggage up into the cargo hold of the plane.

The jet's engines rumbled as they powered up, preparing for takeoff. For the moment, no one was looking this way. But Danny knew if the jet took off, Lawrence and Nadia might be lost forever.

He was quickly running out of time and options.

What would Ryan do?

With sudden inspiration, Danny jumped up onto the conveyer belt. He sprinted up the ramp and dived into the dark abyss of the cargo hold.

CHAPTER

13

**NEW JERSEY,
USA**

I *'m in!*

Ryan looked at Danny's text in confusion, then typed back: *in where? airport?*

the plane. cargo hold.

Ryan stared at the message, not believing it. Danny was on the plane?

r u insane? get out!

Over the deafening roar of the jet's engines, Ryan didn't hear the fuel tanker start up. It began to pull away. Ryan was forced to duck behind the back wheel of the plane.

danny?

Ryan peeked out from behind the tire. On the other side of the plane, he saw the conveyer belt ramp being moved away. The cargo hold had been closed—with Danny trapped *inside*!

Ryan had to make sure this jet didn't take off. He dialed 911, knowing he didn't have much time. At the front of the plane, the passenger stairway was already slowly rising. They were preparing for departure, clearing the area around the aircraft.

"911, what's the nature of your emergency?" said the operator.

"A kidnapping!" Ryan yelled, but the engines were revving up, getting even louder now. The operator said something, but Ryan couldn't make it out. This was useless. It was impossible to hear.

Ryan eyed the back stairway as he disconnected the call. He couldn't leave Danny alone in there.

Thinking fast, he leaned out and shot a photo of the jet's tail section with its distinctive lion's head logo and the numbers that identified each individual plane. Remembering Dad's warning that his parents' phones might not be safe, Ryan texted the picture to Kasey instead. He just hoped she'd figure out what it meant. He only had time to dash off one quick message:

tell my parents we're ok but DON'T TRUST TASHA.

Ryan ran for the stairs that led into the back of the plane. Crouching low, he climbed up, prepared to attack if he ran into one of the crew. But the coast was clear. He was in a kitchen area, sealed off from the rest of the jet. Through a small window, he spotted the flight attendant making her way toward him.

Ryan looked for a place to hide. There were two doors to his right. He opened one and found a small bathroom, probably for the crew. The other revealed a steep spiral staircase leading down. Ryan stepped inside, sliding the door closed just as the flight attendant entered the kitchen. He froze on the metal stairs, keeping absolutely still.

He heard the mechanical rumble of the rear stairway being raised, then the exterior door was locked into place. Ryan's phone buzzed in his pocket as the plane lurched forward. It was probably Kasey wondering what the cryptic text meant. But Ryan couldn't answer it. Both his arms were wedged against the walls as he struggled to keep his balance.

Fighting the motion of the plane, Ryan hurried down the spiral staircase to the lower level. The stairs led to a cargo area, which had been converted for personal use. It was dark down here, so he pulled out his phone and turned on the flashlight app. He was in a pantry that held food, drinks, and supplies. Across from him was a door that he guessed led to the main cargo hold.

Ryan crossed the pantry as the jet swerved, throwing him off-balance again. They must be turning onto the runway. He had to find somewhere to settle in and hold on before he got tossed all over the place.

Beyond the door everything was pitch-black. He went in, flashing the beam of his light across the secured luggage. The plane started racing forward, accelerating by the second.

"Ryan?"

He whipped his light around. Peeking out from behind two equipment cases, Danny stared up at him sheepishly.

"Maybe this wasn't such a great idea," Danny said.

"Ya think?"

Ryan squeezed in next to Danny and held on tight as the jet lifted off, beginning its long trek home to Africa.

CHAPTER
14

**NEW YORK,
USA**

*t*ell my parents we're ok but DON'T TRUST TASHA.

Kasey stared at the text for the hundredth time. The picture Ryan sent was taken from down low and showed the rear of a jet. All she could make out were the tail numbers and a lion's head logo that didn't look like any airline she'd ever seen.

Why wasn't Ryan answering her text? She'd responded immediately, but that was almost an hour ago. It was like he had just disappeared.

She knew Ryan was staying at Danny's this weekend, so she'd texted Danny, too. No response there, either. She tried to look up phone numbers for Ryan's parents, but couldn't find anything online. How was she supposed to tell his parents something when they were out of town and she didn't have their numbers?

Kasey's bedroom door suddenly opened, and her brother Drew appeared. "Hey, did you take my headphones?"

"It's called knocking." Kasey hated it when her brothers or father just barged in. It happened less often now that her two older brothers were away at college, but it was still just as annoying. "And, no, I don't have your headphones."

"Then where are they?"

"How should I know? Maybe Dad borrowed them."

"Dad!" Drew left without closing the door. Kasey got up from her bed and slammed it shut. Her brother had been in a bad mood ever since Lan moved to Washington. From the moment they met, Drew and Lan had been crushing on each other. But now Lan had a new identity and, for her safety, they weren't allowed to contact her. Drew still had a major crush on her, though. He was having a hard time letting go, and he took it out on his family, sulking and picking stupid fights. Kasey tried to be patient, but she still wanted to slap him sometimes.

Kasey was tempted to tell her brother about

the text from Ryan. Drew had helped them out before, and she thought she could trust him. But the moment she considered it, she realized exactly what would happen. Drew would get all bossy, telling her what to do and being over-protective. That's how it had been since Kasey was little. After her mom got sick and died, the Stieglitz men made it their mission to keep her safe and secure. She adored her dad and broth-ers, but they could be suffocating at times.

Kasey was a teenager now. Ryan sent the text message to her, and she didn't need Drew's help to figure out what to do. Ryan was count-ing on Kasey, and she would prove his faith in her wasn't misplaced.

The only clue she had was that picture of the tail fin. There had to be some way to find out more about the plane. Grabbing her lap-top, Kasey searched online and finally located a website that looked promising. She typed in the jet's identifying numbers, excited to discover the plane's registration information was part of the public record.

A company called Sekhmet Technologies owned the jet. She did some research and quickly spotted the lion's head logo from Ryan's photo. Sekhmet operated a collection of cellular and broadband networks in Africa. Their corporate headquarters was in a city called Houdali in the Republic of Lovanda.

Lovanda. The same country where the rapper they met yesterday was going to be executed.

Alarmed now, Kasey looked at the text once more: *tell my parents we're ok but DON'T TRUST TASHA.*

No way. Ryan and Danny couldn't possibly have been that nuts.

Could they?

Kasey jumped up, grabbing her coat. Somehow, she had to find Ryan's parents!

CHAPTER
15

**OVER THE
ATLANTIC OCEAN**

S towing away on an airplane sucks." Danny's teeth chattered as he hugged himself tightly, trying uselessly to keep warm.

Ryan huddled next to him. They were tucked in between the luggage and trunks. A single emergency light emitted a weak glow. "What were you thinking?"

"I guess I wasn't." Danny smiled. "I have made an important realization, though."

"Yeah?"

"When that little voice pops up in my head saying, 'What would Ryan do?'—I should just ignore it."

Ryan grinned back. "I probably should, too."

Danny shifted around, trying to get comfortable on the cold floor. "What're we gonna do when we land?"

"Hide. When everyone's gone, we'll sneak out. Find a phone and contact my parents."

"They're never gonna let me join the ERC after this."

"At least we'll be able to tell them where Lawrence and Nadia are. They can figure out some way to help."

But first, they had to survive the flight.

They'd been traveling for a couple of hours, staying as still as possible. Ryan guessed they had at least another twelve hours to go if they were flying all the way to Lovanda. They needed food, some way to keep warm, and a safe place to hide when they landed.

The cramped cargo hold was metal on all sides, so it was difficult not to make noise. Ryan pulled off his high-tops, then stood. Even in socks, he was careful to step softly. "We're lucky this compartment is pressurized. Otherwise, we would've passed out already."

"Might be better than this." Danny shivered. "And I thought flying coach was bad."

"Stay here."

"Ryan, no—I'm kidding. I'm fine. You can't go out there."

"Ssshh." Ryan carefully turned the metal handle of the cargo door, hoping it wouldn't squeak. It made a soft, metallic click, not loud enough to be heard over the rumbling of the jet's engines. Ryan opened the door and peeked out.

The pantry area was dark and empty. Turning on his phone's flashlight, he slipped out and inspected the pantry shelves. There were containers filled with packaged foods, coffees and teas, and tins of cookies and biscuits. Most of it seemed to have come from England and France. Refrigerated units held uncooked meat, as well as a lot of fresh fruits and vegetables.

But there were no blankets or other supplies down here. Ryan went to the spiral staircase and listened. Hearing nothing, he risked heading up.

At the top of the stairs, he turned off his light and pressed an ear against the door. No sound, no movement from the other side. He slid the pocket door open. Ryan crept out, peering through the window into the main cabin area. The galley kitchen led to a long hallway that was lined with cabinets. Ryan guessed he'd find blankets in one of them.

He had to hurry before the flight attendant returned. Ryan stepped into the hallway and started opening cabinets. The first revealed a variety of small kitchen appliances and utensils. The next was filled with life vests and emergency gear. In the farthest cabinet, Ryan found what he needed: sheets, pillows, and blankets.

"I appreciate that, Madame Buku." Ryan froze at the man's voice. The hallway opened into what looked like a lounge area. The voice was coming from there. Ryan could see several swivel chairs covered in luxurious leather, but no sign of the speaker.

"They say you get what you pay for," the unseen man continued in a lilting British accent. "And since you always pay for the best, I don't like to disappoint."

Ryan crept forward and peered around the edge of the cabinets to get a better view. It was the man with the scar across his face. The leader of the team that took Lawrence and Nadia. His back was now to Ryan as he talked on the phone, sipping a cocktail. He had the cropped hair and muscular physique of a soldier.

"We'll bring Anbo and Delilah directly to your compound. My men and I'll keep an eye on them until Monday morning. Then we'll personally transport them to Liberty Plaza for the execution. You'll finally be able to make an example of them the whole country will witness." He listened a moment. "I assure you, nobody's getting away this time."

Ryan saw a door swinging open from the opposite hallway and ducked back out of sight. He grabbed an armful of blankets, then silently shut the cabinet door.

Behind him, the scarred man finished his call. "We'll see you in the morning, then."

"I thought you might be ready for another drink, Mr. Laughlin." That must be the flight attendant.

"Thanks," said Laughlin, rattling the ice in his glass. "Here's to the upcoming extermination of two more rats."

Ryan wished he could punch the guy.

He slipped back into the kitchen area, closing the door gently behind him, then hurried downstairs. Ryan grabbed fruit, cookies, and cans of tuna from the pantry before returning to the cargo hold.

Danny was worried sick.

"Can you please *never* do that again?" But he stopped, noticing Ryan's grim expression. "What happened?"

"I just heard the lead guy talking. They're planning to execute Lawrence and Nadia. On *Monday*."

"That's less than two days," Danny said, alarmed.

"Yeah. It'll be almost impossible for the ERC to get anybody else to Lovanda in time to help."

The boys were quiet for a moment. Then Danny looked up at Ryan. "You know what this means, right?"

Ryan nodded. "It means this one is up to us."

PART *two*

BACK IN THE GAME

CHAPTER
16

**NEW YORK,
USA**

Kasey had been waiting for almost two hours. She was bored out of her mind. She'd done seven sudoku puzzles, checked Instagram until she was sick of it, and texted some of her friends who were traveling for the holidays. The problem with having a curious mind was that sitting still often seemed like complete torture.

Finally, a dark blue BMW pulled to the curb at the Quinns' brownstone. Ryan's dad got out of the front passenger side and opened the back door for Jacqueline. They both looked tired and worried. Kasey jumped from the stoop, anxious to tell them her fears about Ryan and Danny.

"Kasey . . ." Jacqueline's brow furrowed. "Are you meeting Ryan here? We haven't been able to reach him."

"Me neither. But I think I may know . . ."

Kasey froze as a young woman got out of the driver's side. She had short hair and intense green eyes that focused on Kasey with suspicion. Kasey had never met Tasha before, but felt certain that's who the woman was. She must have picked the Quinns up from the airport. Ryan said not to trust her, so Kasey had to be careful.

"You know where Ryan is?" Jacqueline prompted.

"Yeah." Kasey struggled with what to say, then remembered something her brothers mentioned. "He and Danny went to the Museum of Natural History to see that new 3D movie on sharks. There's no cell reception in there."

John grabbed a small suitcase from the back. "He should've let us know."

"He probably thought he'd be back before you got home." Kasey fought her nerves as Tasha came closer. "Hi! I'm Kasey—we haven't met."

"Tasha." Tasha turned away, dismissive of Kasey like so many of those snotty upper-grade girls at school. Whatever. Kasey wanted as little to do with her as possible, anyway. Tasha followed John up the stairs.

"Would you like to come in until the boys get back?" Jacqueline asked.

Kasey waited until Tasha disappeared inside, then whipped out her phone. "You need to see this."

Puzzled, Jacqueline read the text and examined the tail fin photo. "What does it mean?"

"I think Ryan and Danny may be on that plane."

Jacqueline was confused. "That's impossible. How could they be on a plane?"

"I checked the registration. It's a private jet owned by a company in Lovanda, Africa."

Realization swept over Ryan's mom. "Oh no. That young man you all met last night."

"Lawrence. Ryan told you about him and Nadia, right?"

Jacqueline nodded. "We asked Tasha to check on him at the brownstone this morning. She said there'd been a break-in. That Lawrence was . . ."

But she stopped, looking again at Ryan's message: *DON'T TRUST TASHA.* Jacqueline ran a hand through her long hair, clearly agitated. She looked back up to the door where Tasha had followed John into their home.

"Ryan sent that text, and then I haven't heard from him again." Kasey took the phone back. "Danny, either."

"So the museum—you just made that up?"

"I didn't want to say anything in front of Tasha."

"Smart."

"Ryan specifically said they were okay. I don't think he would've said that if it wasn't true."

"I agree. Which means they may not be in immediate danger. Not yet, anyway."

Kasey could see Jacqueline's mind racing, putting the pieces together and figuring out what to do. Knowing Ryan's parents didn't want them involved, she expected to be sent home. But Jacqueline surprised her.

"I need to talk to John and come up with a plan. Unfortunately, right now I'm not sure who in the ERC we can trust, and I don't think we can do this on our own."

"You can trust me," Kasey said.

"Good. Because somehow, we have to get rid of Tasha without her becoming suspicious, keep Danny's mom from calling the police when he doesn't show up for dinner, and bring Ryan and Danny back home safe from wherever the hell that plane is taking them."

Kasey didn't hesitate. "How can I help?"

CHAPTER
17

**FARAJI PROVINCE,
LOVANDA, AFRICA**

Traveling for so long in the dark cargo hold of the plane was disorienting. Ryan had dozed occasionally, but it was a restless sleep. He was too worried about keeping Danny safe and rescuing Lawrence and Nadia.

He had plenty of other worries, too.

Through the hours, his thoughts kept coming back to the photo album Kasey had found in the study. He realized she was right—there were no pictures of him until he was at least a year old. Ryan couldn't even recall any photos of his mom being pregnant.

Of course, his family traveled around so much that it was possible all those pictures had somehow gotten lost or destroyed. But he couldn't remember Mom or Dad ever mentioning that. You'd think it would've been something that had upset them. Something they would have talked about.

The ear-piercing whine of machinery suddenly filled the metal chamber. Danny jerked up, clenching Ryan's forearm in a death grip.

"Oh my god, we're crashing!"

"Chill, it's just the landing gear." Ryan peeled his friend's fingers from his arm.

"Geez—that is *not* a good way to wake up." Danny rubbed the heels of his palms into his eyes. He'd had no trouble sleeping. "What time is it?"

"If we're landing in Lovanda, it's about nine in the morning." Ryan grabbed one of the thick straps attached to the wall and handed it to Danny. "Wrap that around your arm and hold on tight."

Danny looked queasy. "I'm really more of a window seat kind of guy."

"We'll try to upgrade on the flight home." Ryan offered what he hoped was a reassuring smile just as the plane lurched to the right, flinging them both into the wall. "Think of it like a roller coaster. Hold on!"

"I hate roller coasters!" Danny clung to the

strap as the jet abruptly dipped. The boys lifted off the floor, surprisingly weightless as the jet descended. They slammed back to the hard floor, but never let go.

Several minutes later, the plane touched down. Thankfully, the pilot was skillful and brought them in smoothly.

"Now what?" Danny asked.

"Now we make sure they don't find us." While Danny slept, Ryan had examined the cargo hold. Behind a white plastic tarp attached to the ceiling, he discovered several boxes filled with emergency supplies. It looked like they were kept there permanently, which meant they wouldn't be unloaded. He had created a hiding place among the boxes, just big enough for the two boys to fit inside.

Danny looked at it skeptically. "I know I'm small, but that's insulting."

"The other option is getting shot."

The boys wedged themselves into the tight space as the plane taxied down the runway. By the time the plane stopped and the engines shut off, they were safely hidden away. For long minutes, they waited.

"What I wouldn't give for a toothbrush and a hot shower right now," Danny whispered.

Before Ryan could reply, the cargo door opened. Sunlight flooded in, bright and painful after the hours of darkness. Ryan and Danny closed their eyes and stayed as still as statues while the luggage was removed. The man hoisting the bags came so close they could hear the curses he mumbled under his breath.

Finally, Ryan heard him leave the cargo hold. He risked peeking out. Through the open hatch, he saw a line of white SUVs. Laughlin and his men were loading up. There was no sign of Lawrence and Nadia, but Ryan assumed they were already in one of the vehicles.

When the cars drove away, Ryan pried himself from their hiding place and crept to the opening. The landing strip was in an isolated area, a huge open field with a forest beyond. Jagged mountains rose in the distance. Ryan could only see two buildings: a small control shack outfitted with antennas and a huge hangar for the plane itself.

Only three people were visible. The pilot and copilot walked toward the hangar with another man—probably the guy who unloaded the bags. Ryan didn't see the flight attendant anywhere. She might still be cleaning up the plane.

"Holy crap." Danny was right behind him. His

eyes were wide, and he looked pale. "We're in *Africa*."

"You okay? You're not freaking out, are you?"

"Won't lie. Kinda freaking out. All of a sudden, it got real."

"We'll be fine." Ryan saw the three men disappear into the hangar. "Let's go."

They were taking a chance, but Ryan thought they might not get a better opportunity. He dropped to the ground. Crouching, he scanned the area but didn't see anybody else. Danny landed beside him.

"There!" Ryan pointed to the control shack. He darted across the open field, Danny right on his heels. With every step, he expected to hear someone shout after them. But they made it without being spotted, ducking behind the back of the building. Danny powered up his phone as Ryan peered inside a window.

The shack was empty. But against the wall, Ryan spotted a desk with an older computer and several monitors that looked like radar screens. The walls were filled with maps and charts.

"No cell signal," Danny said.

"There's a computer inside."

Danny looked up at the roof. A satellite dish with the Sekhmet Technologies lion's head logo pointed toward the sky. "They've got internet access, but it's password-protected. I can probably break the encryption, but it'll take time."

"We don't have time." Ryan glanced over and saw the copilot step out of the hangar and head back toward the plane. He pointed across an expanse toward the wooded area. "Run to those trees. Keep quiet, but move fast."

"What are you gonna do?"

"Get a message home. Let them know where we are."

Danny seemed uncertain but did as Ryan asked. Once he made it to the trees, he turned back and gave Ryan a thumbs-up. Ryan confirmed the copilot hadn't seen him, then snuck around to the other side of the shack.

He slipped into the control room. Staying in a crouch so his head wouldn't be seen through the windows, Ryan hurried to the computer. An email program was open, but everything was written in Swahili. Fortunately, Ryan had lived in Africa twice in his life and recognized enough of it to navigate the page.

He composed a brief email for his parents, but addressed it to Kasey as he had the text. Ryan had been a loner most of his life. He'd learned to be self-sufficient, never needing to depend on other people. But he was starting to understand that the ERC's operations weren't possible without people working together. He had to trust that Kasey would get the message to his parents safely. Ryan hit send.

"Hoja ya ndege!" Ryan popped his head up and saw the landing-strip worker exit the hangar, shouting at the copilot. He was heading right for the control shack!

Ryan could possibly knock this guy out. Dad had been training him in Krav Maga, a fighting system developed by the Israeli army, since he was ten years old. But as soon as the unconscious man was discovered, everyone would know he and Danny were here. They had a better chance of helping Lawrence and Nadia if they kept a low profile. He needed a way out.

The back window was big enough to fit through. As Ryan crossed to it, he noticed the maps on the wall again. They detailed this whole area with several spots circled in red marker.

"Nakuja, nakuja!" The worker was almost to the door.

Ryan snapped photos of the maps, not even bothering to frame the shots. He opened the window and leaped through, landing with a thud on his back. Ryan heard the door open inside the control room.

A moment of silence, then footsteps crossed toward the window. Ryan scrambled around the side of the building. He ducked out of sight a split second before the worker arrived. After a moment, the man closed the window.

Across the open stretch, Ryan and Danny shared a look—that was close.

Ryan ran for the shelter of the trees.

CHAPTER
18

**FARAJI PROVINCE,
LOVANDA, AFRICA**

Can we stop for a second?"

They'd been moving at a fast pace through the forest for almost twenty minutes. Ryan saw that Danny was sweating and breathing heavily.

"Sure. I think we're far enough away." Ryan pulled out his phone as Danny sat on a rock. He zoomed in on one of the maps he'd photographed. It showed a satellite image of the whole area. "There's only one road leading away from that airstrip. It goes all the way to a lake. Looks like this is Madame Buku's compound on the shore."

Danny looked at the road anxiously. "How far is it?"

"Over ten miles. But that's the long way around. You have to take that road if you're driving. Since we're on foot, we can cut through this area here." Ryan traced a path with his finger. It was almost a straight line from the airfield to the compound. "It's less than half the distance."

On the satellite image, the forest area they were in showed up as dark green. It was only a small strip on the map, which meant they would be out in the open soon.

"You're sure that's where they took Lawrence and Nadia?" Danny asked.

"Laughlin—that guy with the scar—that's what he said on the phone. They're keeping them at the compound until the execution on Monday."

"Do you really think we can save them?" Danny asked uneasily.

"Not alone." After seeing Laughlin's men, trained mercenaries outfitted with dangerous weapons, Ryan knew he and Danny were out of their league. "We'll get as close as we can. Figure out exactly where they're holding them. Then, we have to find some way to get in touch with my parents and get help."

"Can the ERC deal with something like this? Those dudes look like stone-cold killers."

The truth was, Ryan wasn't sure. There was still so much he didn't know about the ERC and how it worked. But Lawrence said Ryan's grandfather and his associates helped break them out of jail once. Maybe they could do it again.

"We'll find out." Ryan looked off through the trees. "According to the map, there's a small river up ahead. Once we cross that, it's pretty wide-open."

"You know, I always wanted to visit Africa." Danny got to his feet. "Though I was thinking more the luxury hotel and guided safari expedition, not the goons-shooting-at-you-with-semiautomatic-rifles package."

Ryan stood. "This trip's a lot cheaper."

After another ten minutes of walking, the trees thinned out. The sound of running water got louder as forest gave way to scrub and rocks. When they finally emerged from the trees, they were at the top of a small hill. Danny stopped in his tracks.

"Whoa."

The grasslands stretched into the distance for miles in every direction. Clusters of trees dotted the landscape, and a river snaked along the plain. The sun was high overhead, bathing everything in golden light.

"It's like a National Geographic documentary—only real." Danny's voice suddenly shot up an octave. "Oh my god, *giraffes!*"

Ryan followed Danny's gaze. Across the river, two giraffes lazily ate from a tree. Movement to Ryan's left drew his attention.

"Over there—zebras." Ryan pointed across the plain. A small herd of black-and-white-striped steeds grazed together.

Only now did Ryan notice that a fence blocked the bottom of the small hill where they stood. It stretched out in both directions as far as he could see. "I think it's some kind of game reserve."

Danny's eyes lit up. "Madame Buku owns a game reserve! I read about it online. She rescues exotic animals from all over the world."

"Guess she's not all bad."

"I'm not so sure. There are rumors that she invites important people to her private reserve for exotic hunting parties. Some people even say she feeds the animals to her pet lions."

The fence was well built, but it wasn't very high. It was designed to keep the animals in, not to keep people out. They could easily climb it.

"The compound is straight across the

reserve," Ryan said. "If we turn back, we have to go all the way around."

"That'll take hours." Danny regarded the wide-open savanna teeming with wildlife. "Guess I'm gonna get my safari after all."

CHAPTER
19

**KALHIRI PARK,
LOVANDA, AFRICA**

Both times Ryan's family lived in Africa, they had been in large cities. The most recent visit had been a year ago when his dad organized a United Nations outreach program in Cameroon. For a few months, they lived in Douala, a bustling, chaotic industrial hub.

Ryan had been surprised and impressed. It wasn't the Africa shown in movies and TV shows. There weren't warlords with AK-47s or tribal elders with exotic piercings and tattoos. The city was full of people of all types. Kids going to school and to the mall, parents working office jobs, old men gathering in the park telling stories from their youth.

Africa was ancient, but it was embracing the modern age. There were plenty of places with serious problems, but even more that were growing and prospering. It seemed like the rest of the world didn't care much about that side of Africa, though. Only the strange, mysterious, and dangerous aspects of the vast continent got attention.

Making his way across the unspoiled wilderness of the reserve, Ryan recognized that this was the Africa outsiders fantasized about: extraordinary animals, stunning scenery, and not a car or building in sight.

"It's like the world's most awesome zoo, but with no cages," Danny said. "And no bathrooms. Which I could really use right now."

"There're plenty of bushes." Ryan gestured to the clumps of trees along the river. "And leaves."

"Ew. I'll hold it."

"There's no one around for miles."

"Your family may be the survive-in-the-wilderness, the-world-is-my-bathroom type. But I grew up in Manhattan. We prefer a locked door and two-ply tissue."

"Maybe the elephants have some toilet paper you can borrow?"

Ryan gestured toward a rise where two elephants were just coming up from the river below. They were small, probably pygmy elephants, with huge ears and gorgeous tusks. And they weren't afraid at all. In fact, they marched right toward Ryan and Danny.

"Stay still," Ryan said. "They're just curious."

Danny's expression wavered between astonishment and terror as one of the elephants stopped in front of him. It lifted its trunk and began exploring Danny's face. The trunk touched his ear, then slid along his chin, leaving a trail of wet, sticky goo.

"So disgusting," Danny whispered as Ryan laughed.

The trunk traced circles around Danny's nose, the elephant seemingly fascinated by this strange and very small appendage. The second elephant made a sudden noise like a trumpet blast, then they both ran off as quickly as they'd come.

"Guess they didn't like the taste of you."

Danny grinned as he turned, wiping the gross mess from his face. But he abruptly froze, staring over Ryan's shoulder.

"It wasn't me they didn't like."

Ryan spun around. Less than thirty feet

away, a powerhouse of muscle and armored skin stared at him with beady, black eyes. The rhino snorted angrily, its lethal horns lowered and pointed directly at Ryan. The ears on top of its head pivoted forward, and the beast stomped one giant leg against the ground.

Danny gulped. "Run!"

CHAPTER

20

**KALHIRI PARK,
LOVANDA, AFRICA**

T he rhino charged, moving faster than Ryan imagined possible for such a gigantic creature. The spiked horn on its massive head was aimed right at Ryan's gut.

"Get behind the trees!" he yelled to Danny.

The rhino covered the distance quickly. Ryan had to time this perfectly. When the armor-plated beast was ten feet away, Ryan dropped his shoulder and dived to the right. He rolled across the ground twice to make sure he was out of the way as the rhino thundered past.

Leaping to his feet, Ryan was surprised to see a second rhino emerge from the river. A baby. The giant rhino was simply protecting its young. Unfortunately, knowing that wouldn't keep Ryan from getting killed.

The papa rhino turned around and got Ryan in his sights again. Ryan sprinted away as the pounding of the rhino's hooves came closer by the moment.

"Aaaaaggghhhh!!!" Emerging from behind a tree, Danny screamed, waving his arms frantically to distract the beast. The rhino stopped, facing Danny.

As Ryan darted past, Danny threw a rock. It bounced off the tough skin harmlessly. The rhino grunted angrily, and Danny hurried to join Ryan behind the trees.

But the trees lining the banks of the river were too thin and sparse to stop a charging rhino. It snorted and moved closer, tracking the boys with dark eyes.

"Maybe it'll just go away," Danny whispered.

"Maybe." But Ryan wasn't hopeful, watching the baby lumber up behind the bigger rhino.

For a couple of tense minutes, the rhino remained fixated on the cluster of trees where they hid. Abruptly, it turned away, ears pivoting. Another sound could barely be detected now. Engines, getting closer.

Two all-terrain vehicles suddenly surged over the small slope that rose up from the river, each ridden by a man in fatigues and a black helmet. They revved the four-wheeled dirt bikes, spinning to a stop on opposite sides of the rhino. They had rifles strapped to their backs, which they pulled into position.

Crack-crack! Ryan instinctively grabbed Danny, yanking him to the ground as the two shots rang out. The rhino staggered, bullets piercing its hide, as the ATVs raced off once more.

Danny couldn't believe it. "They're trying to kill it."

"Poachers." Ryan's tone was grim. Poachers were scum, preying on some of the most endangered animals in the world. These guys would kill the rhinos, then cut off their horns to sell on the black market. "They'll shoot the baby, too."

The rhino turned toward one of the four-wheelers as two more shots rang out. It bellowed, hit once more in the shoulder, then charged again. The ATVs were old and beat-up, but the rhino was still no match for their speed. The men slid the rifles onto their backs and zoomed away, getting into position for another round of shots.

The baby wandered in a daze, circling in confusion. When Ryan saw one of the poachers closing in on it, he stood. Desperate to help, he examined the tree. He spotted a long, sturdy branch that could work for what he had in mind and broke it off.

"What are you doing?"

"Probably something stupid," Ryan admitted. With swift movements, he snapped the smaller sticks from the main branch. When he'd visited Tahiti one summer, Ryan became friends with a kid who worked at the Polynesian Cultural Center. The boy's summer job was showing tourists the traditional sport of spear throwing. He and Ryan had hung out for a couple of weeks, and Ryan had thrown tons of javelins before his family left.

Danny eyed the spear dubiously. "I hope you're not gonna joust with him."

As the poacher zeroed in on the rhino baby, Ryan emerged from the safety of the trees. He didn't take time to think. He just let his body do the work, remembering what throwing all those spears felt like. At the moment the ATV came closest to him, he let the spear fly.

The branch wobbled terribly as it sailed through the air. The throw was low and a moment too late. Ryan had aimed for the rider's body, but missed!

Startled by the flying object, the poacher turned to see where it had come from. Ryan was now completely exposed. But the momentary distraction accomplished what Ryan's spear throwing hadn't.

The man wasn't watching where he was going as one of his front tires hit a large rock. The ATV went up on two wheels, then completely flipped onto its side. The shocked rider was flung from the bike. He crashed to the ground with a thud.

As the poacher groggily tried to get up and unstrap his rifle, Ryan ran toward him. With one swift motion, he picked up his improvised spear and swung it, whacking the man against the side of his helmet. The poacher collapsed to the ground, unconscious.

Ryan looked up at the baby rhino. "Go! Shoo!"

"Ryan, look out!" Danny yelled from behind.

The second poacher had seen what happened and was now gunning for Ryan. He braked to a skidding stop and pulled his rifle from his back. He snapped the bolt, chambering a round. Raised the weapon and aimed at Ryan when—

BAM! The daddy rhino plowed into the ATV. The man, the gun, and the machine all went flying. The poacher landed so hard his helmet was knocked off. The rhino lowered its head and charged the battered ATV once more, spearing it and ripping the four-wheeler apart.

Ryan didn't waste any time. He pulled the helmet off the guy at his feet and put it on. Grunting with effort, he wrestled the ATV back upright, then threw a leg over the seat.

Ryan pressed the starter and pulled back on the throttle. The ATV roared to life. Ryan motioned to Danny.

"Get on!"

"You ridden one of those before?"

"Not exactly. But I drove a Jet Ski—it can't be that different, right?"

"Snow and dirt. Completely different."

Ryan revved the engine. "You can always stay and play chicken with the rhino."

Grudgingly, Danny climbed onto the back. The rhino turned to engage them once more. But Ryan had no intention of facing the colossal beast again.

He twisted the gas and the four-wheeler lurched forward.

Then it instantly died, the engine sputtering out.

"Don't say a word," Ryan warned Danny. As the rhino started toward them, he pressed the starter and twisted the throttle again. After the engine caught, he accelerated gradually, slowly gaining speed.

Ryan gave the rhino a wide berth. As they passed the downed ATV, he stopped long enough to scoop up the second poacher's discarded helmet. Danny strapped it on, and they raced away.

CHAPTER
21

**NEW YORK,
USA**

H ow's this?"

Kasey turned from the mirror to face Jacqueline. Her blonde curls were tucked inside a wig of straight black hair. The short, severe cut made Kasey look a lot older than an eighth grader.

"Almost perfect." Jacqueline handed her a pair of trendy eyeglasses, and Kasey put them on. "There. Now, you look like a thousand other young women on the streets of New York."

Morning sun slanted through the windows in the back room of Jacqueline's store. Kasey had never been here before and wished she had more time to explore. The elegant shop was filled with rare musical instruments, some of them hundreds of years old, that Ryan's mom bought and sold around the world. It was a great cover job for ERC missions, allowing Jacqueline the perfect excuse to travel anywhere she was needed.

The back room was an unfinished space crowded with spare instrument parts and packing supplies. Jacqueline had spread out a collection of jackets, scarves, and hats on a worktable. Several Styrofoam heads displayed wigs in a variety of styles and colors.

"The key to following someone," Jacqueline told her, "is to never let them see the same person twice. That means always changing your look. A new hat or jacket and you'll appear completely different to your target."

Their target would be Tasha.

Jacqueline had been very conflicted about letting Kasey get more involved. But Kasey had pressed her case: What if Jacqueline called someone else in the ERC to help, and they were actually working with Tasha? The element of surprise was the greatest advantage they had in finding out who Tasha was working with and preventing more people from being exposed or killed. Until Jacqueline knew for sure who could be trusted, Kasey insisted that she was the safest choice.

Her argument finally swayed Jacqueline. She agreed to let Kasey help so long as she did exactly as instructed. They'd stop immediately if Jacqueline even suspected Kasey might be exposed to danger. Kasey promised to be careful and only do what Jacqueline said.

So far, things had gone well.

Kasey accomplished her first task yesterday afternoon, right after telling Ryan's mom about Tasha. Jacqueline had asked her to come inside the brownstone and pretend to wait for Ryan. From the kitchen, Kasey could hear Tasha and John talking downstairs. She tried to relax and act casual, but couldn't stop glancing at the stairway, waiting anxiously for Tasha to appear.

Jacqueline had come back, whispering that she had a job for her. Kasey looked down at the tiny electronic device Jacqueline pressed into her palm.

"It's a magnetic GPS tracker. I need you to attach it inside the back wheel well of Tasha's car. Can you do that?"

"Sure." Kasey felt her heart beating faster.

"I'll call you when Tasha's gone," Jacqueline said. "We'll figure out what to do next."

Kasey had been impressed with how calm and determined Jacqueline seemed. Only minutes before, she'd learned her son was probably half a world away and that a woman she thought of as an ally was really their enemy. Kasey could see how worried Jacqueline was, but Ryan's mom kept her cool and made a plan.

In front of the brownstone, Kasey made sure no one was looking, then placed the transmitter inside the back wheel well. Quick as a flash, her first assignment was done. Easy.

For a little while, it felt like a fun game. Like being a real-life spy. But an hour later, after Tasha had left and Kasey was back downstairs with Jacqueline and John, the urgency of the situation became clear.

Ryan had been right to think that something bad was going on. The Quinns revealed to Kasey that people the ERC had rescued were starting to disappear. One had even been killed. If they didn't find out who was responsible and stop them, more would be in danger.

Jacqueline and John both agreed that their

priority was finding Ryan and Danny and bringing them home. But someone had to stay focused on stopping the leak inside the ERC. They decided that Ryan's dad would go to Africa while Jacqueline stayed behind to deal with the ERC problem. John booked a seat on the next flight to Lovanda as his wife called Danny's mom.

Kasey marveled at how skillfully Jacqueline transformed. Speaking with Mrs. Santiago, Jacqueline was bubbly and cheerful. While they were visiting Chicago, she said, a friend offered them his cabin up in the Adirondack Mountains for a few days. Was it okay if Danny came along? Mrs. Santiago was delighted, especially when Jacqueline added that she was instituting a strict no cell phones policy for the trip.

No cell phones meant Mrs. Santiago wouldn't try to get in touch with Danny. Jacqueline thought of everything!

"That was amazing," Kasey said. "You just came up with all that out of thin air."

But Jacqueline was subdued, her carefree facade gone. "Lying to people you care about never feels amazing. It usually makes you feel pretty terrible."

With his flight departing in fewer than three hours, John had to leave right away. He packed quickly and headed out. At the door, Kasey watched as he hugged Jacqueline, promising to update her as often as possible.

"Why would Ryan do something so dangerous?" he asked.

"Are you really surprised?" Jacqueline replied. "It's in his blood."

John nodded and sighed, then left.

By then, it was getting late and Kasey had to head home. Jacqueline said she'd keep track of Tasha for the night. They still had no idea why Ryan didn't trust her. Was Tasha the leak inside the ERC? And if she was, were other members working with her? Jacqueline explained to Kasey that she didn't have the capability to tap Tasha's phone, but they could follow her and try to learn more about what she was doing. However, it took at least two people to effectively tail someone without getting spotted. Kasey volunteered to meet Jacqueline early the next morning.

The excitement of taking part in the operation faded overnight, though. Kasey hardly slept, tossing and turning. She worried that she'd mess up and couldn't stop wondering if Ryan and Danny were okay. Kasey's imagination often got the better of her. She envisioned a million different ways things could go wrong. By the time she woke, Kasey was a mess, filled with indecision and doubt.

Checking her phone, Kasey was confused to see an email from someone named Samuli Baako. She was about to delete it when she noticed the first line: MOM & DAD—SORRY. It was from Ryan! The message was brief, confirming Kasey's belief that they were in Lovanda and assuring his parents they were being cautious. They were following the men who took Lawrence and Nadia. Ryan said the couple was going to be held at a house owned by a woman named Evelyn Buku.

Kasey jumped out of bed. Clearly, Ryan trusted her to get the message to his parents. She wouldn't let him down.

Kasey texted Jacqueline that it was important they meet at her shop as soon as possible. Jacqueline responded immediately, giving Kasey the address. As she hurried out, Kasey kissed her dad on the cheek and promised to check in during the day.

Running the whole way, Kasey found the musical instrument shop quickly. Inside, Jacqueline read the email from Ryan and fought back tears. Watching her, Kasey saw how hard it really was for Ryan's mom to keep her emotions under control.

After a moment, Jacqueline pulled herself together and turned to Kasey. "Would you still like to help?"

"Of course. Whatever you need."

"Then let's get you changed."

Now, standing there in the back of the store, Kasey looked in the mirror, barely recognizing herself in the short hair and glasses that Jacqueline had given her. She still felt nervous and uncertain. But Ryan and his mom both seemed to have faith in her, so she'd better have it in herself.

"Tasha's on the move," Jacqueline said, snapping Kasey out of her reverie. "You navigate, I'll drive."

Jacqueline handed Kasey a smartphone. On its screen, a blinking dot hovered over a map of Manhattan. The dot was moving along Park Avenue.

"She's headed north," Kasey reported.

"Grab a jacket and hat in case we have to

follow her on foot." Jacqueline opened the back door as Kasey scooped up several items. "You ready for this?"

After a quick adjustment of her wig, Kasey nodded. "Let's go."

CHAPTER
22

**LAKE TARU,
LOVANDA, AFRICA**

The ATV roared down the two-lane road. Even though it was December, it was hot here, the afternoon sun baking Ryan and Danny as they traveled along the asphalt.

To their left, a sprawling shantytown extended in all directions. Flimsy huts built from sheets of corrugated metal were packed together with no sense of order. Dust from the dirt roads created a haze that hung in the still air. Ryan had seen a lot of extreme poverty in his travels, and he never got used to it. It made him mad that people had to live like this in the modern world.

"There's a turnoff a couple of miles ahead," Danny yelled, consulting the photo of the map. "That'll take us to the lake."

They continued along the road, cresting a small hill. Coming down the other side, the shantytown vanished from view, and the deep-blue waters of the lake appeared in the distance. The opposite shore was lined by the jagged peaks of a mountain range. It was beautiful, Ryan thought, so unspoiled. Only a few miles separated the shantytown from the lake, but they seemed to exist in two different worlds.

"There!" Danny pointed to an intersection up ahead.

Ryan took the turn and followed a smaller road toward the water. For several minutes, they wound around the lake's perimeter, rising up and down over rolling terrain. As they reached the top of a hill, a walled complex came into view below.

"That must be it," Danny said. Ryan pulled the ATV off the road and parked behind some bushes. Using trees for cover, the boys climbed uphill to get a better view.

The compound was made up of a collection of buildings spread over several acres along the lake's shoreline. Golden lion heads adorned the front gates. The main residence was an ornate chateau with columns and gold-leaf decoration. A fountain in the middle of the circular driveway spewed water high into the air.

"It's like she built her own Palace of Versailles," Danny marveled.

But Ryan's focus was on the armed guards patrolling the entrance gates. He saw two out front, both carrying submachine guns, and assumed there'd be many more inside. The walls that surrounded the compound looked about ten feet high and were topped with security cameras at regular intervals. Getting in without being spotted would be tricky.

"I'm gonna move closer and try to figure out if Lawrence and Nadia are inside."

"Not without me."

"It's too risky. Stay here. I'll find a way in."

Danny stepped in front of Ryan. "Have you *never* seen a horror movie? When friends split up, terrible things happen. We stick together. End of discussion."

Ryan was surprised at Danny's determination. "Fine. But no doing crazy stuff this time, okay?"

"Deal."

They skirted the edge of the property until Ryan was certain they were out of the guards' view. Keeping low, he and Danny ran to the wall, then followed it toward the lake. Ryan hoped they might discover some place to sneak in from the rear where the cameras wouldn't see them.

They reached the end of the wall, which was only a few feet from the lake's edge. Ryan peered around the corner. He was disappointed to see that the property wasn't open to the water. Even back here, the security wall continued all the way across the shoreline, interrupted only by a closed entry gate.

Danny glanced up. "What's that buzzing?"

Now Ryan heard it, too. The sound was getting closer. Ryan looked at the lake, examining the docks that backed up to Madame Buku's home. One of them was a perfect circle surrounded by water. A long walkway connected it to the shore.

"It's a landing pad!" Ryan grabbed Danny and pulled him down. "Press against the wall—don't move."

Moments later, a helicopter *whooshed* past. The sleek blue chopper looped around, its roar deafening as the downdraft buffeted the boys. Slowly, it made its way to the helipad.

Ryan crawled forward for a better view. A staff member in a crisp white shirt and black pants emerged through the gate and hurried along the dock to the chopper. Several guards with submachine guns followed, watching the arrival. Finally, the helicopter landed and the back door opened. A striking African woman got out. She wore a turquoise gown that touched the ground, her hair covered in an elaborate head wrap the same color as the dress. The wind from the still-spinning blades forced her to hold the headpiece down as she disembarked.

"That's her." Danny was right beside Ryan. "Madame Buku."

With a slight bow, the valet took a briefcase from Madame Buku. She moved toward the gate, where the guards snapped to attention. Everyone's focus was on their boss's arrival. Ryan guessed this might be the best chance to get in unnoticed. He looked up at a security camera atop the wall, then picked up a rock.

"What are you doing?"

"Hopefully, throwing a well-aimed fastball."

Ryan whipped the rock at the security camera, hitting it squarely and smashing the lens. The noise of the chopper drowned out the shattering of glass.

"Nice!" Danny exclaimed.

Ryan shrugged. "Lucky for us I'm better at baseball than I am at basketball." He looked at the wall. "You remember when we had to climb the rope in PE last month?"

Danny's shoulders slumped. "Yeah, I sucked at it."

"Well, that's not an option today. We have to move fast before someone notices the camera's broken. Put your back against the wall and give me a boost."

Danny braced himself, joining his hands together to create a place for Ryan's foot. Ryan backed up, then ran toward Danny.

"Hold tight!"

"Maybe this isn't such a good idea—"

Before he could finish, Ryan planted a shoe in Danny's interlaced hands and catapulted himself as high as he could. He grabbed hold of the top and hoisted himself up, throwing one leg over to the other side.

He'd made it. Now, he just had to get Danny up. Hugging the wall with his legs, he reached back down.

"Grab my hand," he urged.

Danny backed up to get a running start. "What if I fall?"

"You won't!"

Danny took a deep breath, then ran and

jumped. Planting a foot on the wall, he sprung up and stretched for Ryan's outstretched arm. The boys clasped hands, Ryan anchoring himself on the ledge.

"Now climb!"

Danny clutched at Ryan's jeans, struggling to lift himself up. He clawed Ryan's shirt, slowly making his way to the top. When he accidentally yanked a handful of hair, Ryan yelped.

"Sorry," Danny muttered. But with Ryan's help, he finally managed to scale the wall.

Over the water, the helicopter took off once more and flew away. The reverberation of the blades faded as Ryan and Danny dropped into the compound.

They were in.

CHAPTER
23

**LAKE TARU,
LOVANDA, AFRICA**

Danny tried to hide how scared he was. He thought he was keeping a pretty brave face, but inside his stomach was churning.

Please god, don't let me puke, he prayed.

For some reason, he kept thinking about his family. Wondering if his parents were worried sick, not knowing where he was. Or if he'd ever come back. He hated that he might be responsible for making them feel like that. Danny was surprised how much he missed his *nanay* and *tatay*. He even missed Analyn and Lilibeth, which was a total shocker.

Danny had no business being here. He was holding Ryan back. Maybe he should've just stayed with the motorbike and let Ryan do this on his own.

At least getting around unnoticed in the compound wasn't too hard. There were plenty of buildings and the grounds were lush with landscaping. Lots of places to hide.

But also lots of places to keep two captives.

"Look," Ryan said, pointing. "That's Laughlin."

The mercenary with the scar was walking from the front of the property back toward the main house. His coat was off, exposing a shoulder holster that contained a powerful-looking gun. Laughlin whistled a cheerful tune, relaxed and easygoing.

"I bet he's going to report to Madame Buku." Danny studied the path Laughlin was walking, which looped around the perimeter of the property. "So maybe he's coming from wherever Lawrence and Nadia are being held."

Ryan nodded. "Good thinking. Let's check."

Danny felt a little boost of confidence. Maybe he wasn't so terrible at this after all.

Staying concealed behind a row of bushes that lined the path, Danny followed Ryan. They came to a long two-story building, a coach house that faced the road out front. The bottom floor was a huge garage with spaces for at least ten cars. The SUVs from the airstrip were parked in the driveway and a couple of Laughlin's men hung around, talking and laughing. A cobblestone driveway curved away from the garage, leading to a separate entrance for the vehicles.

"It looks like there are rooms upstairs," Ryan whispered. "I bet that's where they're keeping Lawrence and Nadia."

Danny saw the staircase on the side of the building that led to the second floor. At the top, another of Laughlin's men guarded the door that led inside.

"So what do we do?" Danny really hoped the next words to come out of Ryan's mouth wouldn't be "break them out."

"Get out of here and get a message to my parents. Hope they can organize some kind of rescue." Danny breathed a sigh of relief as Ryan watched the men. "Those guys are pros. They'll shoot first and ask questions later."

Danny pulled out his phone. He had less than a third of his battery left, but there was a strong signal here. When he tried to access the internet, though, he was disappointed.

"This system's password-protected, too." Danny looked back at the main residence. Two of the Sekhmet satellite dishes were visible on top of the chateau's roof. "If I could get to one of their computers, I could hack in."

"Reilly, you copy?" Laughlin's voice crackled from a radio sitting on the hood of an SUV.

One of the men grabbed it. "Go for Reilly."

"Change of plans," Laughlin said. "We move the prisoners to the city tonight. Make sure everyone's ready."

"Copy that." The man named Reilly yelled to the others, "Don't bother unpacking. We're taking them to the jail in Houdali."

The other men groaned, then moved off. Reilly followed.

Danny could see Ryan deliberating. His friend glanced up at the windows of the rooms over the garage. Danny knew what he was thinking: Time was running out for Lawrence and Nadia.

"Ryan, get me in the house," Danny said. "We'll find a computer. It's the only way we'll get a message to the ERC soon enough for them to help."

Ryan finally nodded. "Okay. But I've got a bad feeling about this."

Not exactly the encouragement Danny hoped for.

CHAPTER

24

**NEW YORK,
USA**

As they drove through the streets of Manhattan, Kasey received a crash course in surveillance techniques from Jacqueline. Her head was swimming with all the new information.

"It's not about being a master of disguise," Jacqueline instructed. "Shadowing is about blending in. Do it right, and she'll never know you're there."

"Okay."

"You always want to keep several people between you and your target. Pick out something they're wearing that's easily identifiable—a bright scarf or distinctive hat. Their coat, maybe. Something you can keep in your peripheral vision without having to look directly at them."

Kasey recognized this as one of the lessons Ryan's parents had secretly taught him growing up. "It's like 'Follow-the-Monkey.'"

Jacqueline was surprised. "You know about that?"

"Ryan told me all about the games you played with him. I wish my dad had played those kind of games with me."

"Be glad he didn't," Jacqueline said. "The problem with having certain skills is that you feel compelled to use them. Even when you probably shouldn't. I imagine that's why Ryan ended up in the mess he's in now."

Kasey heard the worry in her tone. "Mr. Quinn will find him. He'll bring Ryan and Danny back."

Jacqueline shifted in her seat, craning her neck to look ahead. "Tasha's pulling over again."

Jacqueline drove a nondescript sedan she'd rented, always staying a couple of car lengths behind Tasha. Using the GPS tracker, they had caught up to the BMW easily. So far, Tasha had driven uptown to a diner where she had parked and then gone inside. Jacqueline had left Kasey in the car, then inched up to the picture windows out front. After confirming that Tasha was eating alone and not meeting anyone, they'd waited in the car until she was on the move again.

Tasha drove to the other side of Central Park, parking her car and getting out once more. Jacqueline looked around but realized there was no place for her to park.

"You'll have to follow her until I can find a space." She stopped the car. "Stay in touch, and I'll catch up shortly. We'll trade off, just the way we discussed."

Kasey took a deep breath, then opened the door. She didn't head right for Tasha. Instead, she moved into a small group of people walking past, mingling among them. Safely concealed, she could observe Tasha from a distance.

Remembering Jacqueline's advice, Kasey focused on the camel-brown color of Tasha's distressed leather jacket. A black hoodie sticking out of the collar created a stark contrast that was easy to see in a crowd. Dialing Jacqueline, Kasey hurried to keep up as Tasha disappeared around the corner.

"She turned onto Columbus," Kasey reported. "Heading north."

"I'll drive up a couple of blocks. Let me know if she changes course."

As Kasey disconnected, Tasha suddenly

stopped and started to turn around. Not wanting to be spotted, Kasey switched directions. Don't look back, she cautioned herself. She crossed the street to the opposite side, then glanced back.

Tasha was gone.

How could she just disappear? Kasey hurried to the end of the block, scanning the sidewalks in every direction. But Tasha was nowhere to be seen. Kasey had screwed up. She'd lost the target.

Calm down. Think.

This block of Columbus Avenue was mostly brick apartment buildings with smaller markets and boutiques at the street level. Tasha could have popped into one of the stores. Or she might have gone up to an apartment.

Kasey studied the spot where she'd last seen Tasha. There were two little restaurants close by, one served sushi and another pizza. Tasha had just eaten, so probably not those. An antiques shop displayed a collection of swords and knives in its windows, while a corner market offered fruit and fresh flowers. There was also a single glass door between them, which looked like the entrance to the apartments upstairs.

Just in case Tasha had noticed her, Kasey put

on the gray knit cap she'd brought and took off her coat. Voilà—instant change. Crossing back to the other side of the street, she checked out the market. Two older women talked to an Asian grocer, but otherwise it was empty.

She stopped at the apartment entrance and peered through the glass door. No one was in the lobby or on the stairs that led up to the apartments. Kasey moved on to the antiques store. As she reached for the handle, the door unexpectedly opened, and Tasha stormed out.

"Jerk," she muttered, then headed back the way she'd come without even glancing at Kasey. Following from a distance, Kasey quickly dialed Jacqueline.

"I just found a space," Jacqueline started, but Kasey cut her off.

"I think she's going back to her car!"

Jacqueline cursed, surprising Kasey. "I'll circle around."

Kasey noticed that Tasha was now carrying a large envelope. It was stuffed pretty full, tucked under Tasha's arm protectively. She definitely didn't have it before she went into the shop. Which meant that Tasha had met with someone inside.

Acting on impulse, Kasey returned to the

store and went in. As the door closed behind her, the commotion of the city was silenced, replaced by soft classical music. Rows of old-fashioned wooden display cabinets lined the walls. Down the middle of the store was a long table piled high with timeworn books and catalogs. An imposing antique desk anchored the far end, but no one sat there. The entire place was empty.

The cabinets were filled with weapons of every shape and sort: eighteenth-century dueling pistols, Civil War sabers, ornamental Japanese daggers, medieval axes and pikes. A dazzling gold belt buckle caught her eye. Kasey took a closer look. She was appalled to see that it was adorned with the winged eagle and swastika symbol of the Nazi Party. German Luger pistols from World War II were displayed alongside it.

"You have a keen eye." Kasey turned as a man approached from the back. "Memorabilia from the Third Reich is getting increasingly difficult to procure."

He was completely bald and wore a polka-dotted bow tie and a tweed suit. The man scrutinized her like she was a bug under a microscope. He appeared harmless enough, but something about him made Kasey's skin crawl. If he was the one who gave Tasha the envelope, she had to be careful.

"I've never seen anything like that," Kasey said, pretending to have an interest in the buckle once more.

"Would you like to hold it? That treasure once belonged to a rather prominent Nazi captain." He was obviously proud of it.

"I think I'll pass. But thanks."

"Then how can I help you?"

"I'm, um, Christmas shopping for my dad," she improvised. Kasey had told her father she'd be Christmas shopping all day today, and sticking with the truth as much as possible seemed like the best bet. "He's really into this old stuff."

"Were you looking for anything in particular?" The man in the bow tie was losing patience. Kasey felt her phone vibrate in her coat pocket but ignored it. She needed to get this guy's name before she left.

"Daddy just loves knights and chivalry and all that," she said, trying to sound like a spoiled rich kid. "Mom wants to buy him an authentic suit of armor for Christmas."

He was interested now. "You know, a suit of

armor is expensive. Twenty thousand dollars or more."

"Is that all?" Kasey hoped she was convincing. "Unfortunately, it doesn't look like you have any."

"They're not particularly popular in Manhattan." He took a small case from his jacket pocket and extracted a business card. "But I pride myself on being able to find whatever my clients desire."

Kasey took the card. "Then I should totally have my mom give you a call."

"I'll look forward to it."

"Thanks—bye!" Kasey hurried out of the store, anxious to get away from the distasteful man. When she was outside, she read the business card:

BRAXTON CRISP
Acquisitions & Information
All Inquiries Strictly Confidential

Her cell vibrated again. She answered, already hustling down the street. "Sorry, I couldn't pick up. But I think I may know who Tasha is working with."

CHAPTER
25

**LAKE TARU,
LOVANDA, AFRICA**

I t's creepy in here."

Ryan couldn't agree more. Madame Buku's home was like a museum. The whole place was crammed with antiques. Flowery paper covered the walls and crystal chandeliers hung from every ceiling. The eeriest part was how empty the place was. Cavernous rooms and long hallways with nobody in sight.

Since they'd climbed in through an open window, Ryan had seen only a few scattered staff workers. They were all dressed in the same white shirt and black pants as the valet, moving through the house as silently as ghosts. The chateau was vast, but it seemed like Madame Buku might be the only person actually living here.

So far, they had covered most of the first floor and found nothing. Ryan cautiously opened each door, checking for a computer or phone. Each room was painstakingly decorated in period furnishings. It was like stepping back in time to the 1700s. And in keeping with the theme, there were almost no signs of technology anywhere. For a woman who owned a high-tech company, Madame Buku was definitely stuck in the past.

"The faucets are made of gold!" Danny whispered, popping out of a bathroom.

"Nothing but the best for Madame Buku."

"But I have a question: Flush or don't flush?"

"You can't. They'd hear it all over the house."

"That's what I figured. Kinda gross, though."

Ryan froze, hearing footsteps approach from around the corner. "Quick—back inside."

"Bad idea," Danny whispered.

Ryan pushed him into the bathroom, then carefully closed the door. The smell hit him immediately. He looked at Danny, wrinkling his nose.

"I know, man." Danny glanced at the toilet. "That's why I asked."

After the soft pads of rubber-soled shoes passed by in the hallway, they left the bathroom and resumed their search. The end of the hall opened into a high-ceilinged entryway. The front doors were colossal and gleamed with gold plating. Two gaudy marble staircases curved up on each side of the foyer, leading to the upper floor.

Through a set of open double doors on the opposite side of the vestibule, the boys could see bookshelves and leather club chairs.

"That looks like a library or something," Danny suggested.

"Or an office."

The entryway was wide-open with no place to hide. Crossing it would leave them exposed for several seconds. But the whole place was so freakishly quiet that Ryan decided it was worth the risk.

"I'll go first. Wait here till I signal." Ryan checked to make sure the coast was clear, then darted across the marble floor. He had to fight the urge to stop and stare at the sheer extravagance of it all: Grecian statues peered down from lofty perches and the ceilings looked like Michelangelo himself had painted them.

Ryan poked his head inside the library and saw it was empty. He gestured to Danny, who ran and joined him. Inside, they hit pay dirt.

"Finally!" An ornate desk was situated in front

of a bank of monitors. Several played muted newscasts from around the world, but Danny's attention was focused on a high-end computer system sitting atop the desk. As he plopped into the rolling chair, his fingers started flying over the keyboard.

Ryan closed the open doors. "Send the message to Kasey, but I'll also give you email addresses for my mom and dad. We have to make sure somebody gets it."

"Aren't you afraid of alerting whoever's leaking the ERC information?"

"We have to take the chance. If the ERC can't rescue Lawrence and Nadia tonight, it'll be too late." Ryan spotted the phone on Madame Buku's desk and grabbed it. "I'll call Dad, too."

"I'm telling them the execution is scheduled for tomorrow at Liberty Plaza in Houdali, right?"

"Right." Ryan had just dialed the international access code for the United States when he heard voices. Somebody was right outside the doors and coming closer. Ryan slammed down the phone. "Behind the couch!"

Ryan and Danny barely made it to the long, flowery sofa, ducking behind it as the door opened.

"All I'm saying is why make the same mistake

you made when they were arrested the first time?"

"Because public executions are an excellent deterrent." This was a woman's voice, smooth and refined, with an aristocratic British accent. Ryan and Danny exchanged a look—that must be Madame Buku! "There have been too many protests lately. It's not good for business. The deaths of Anbo and Delilah will encourage obedience."

"But dead is dead. If I take care of it tonight, there's no chance anything goes wrong tomorrow." Ryan couldn't believe how offhand Laughlin sounded as he discussed killing two innocent people.

Madame Buku was having none of it, though. "Nothing will go wrong. I've paid more than enough to the government officials to ensure the executions go as planned."

Laughlin sunk into the couch. He was less than a foot away from Ryan and Danny. "Speaking of payment . . ."

"I assume gold will be acceptable?"

Laughlin chuckled. "Gold's my favorite color."

Ryan was unexpectedly overwhelmed by the anger he felt. They were both so coldhearted and uncaring. Laughlin was a thug who did anything for money. Madame Buku was even worse, using her wealth and power to keep everyone else down.

"Gold, it is," she said. "Make yourself comfortable. We're going to be here for a little while."

Fuming behind the sofa, Ryan heard the door open and shut as Madame Buku left the room. Without even thinking about what he was doing, he stood up behind Laughlin.

Rage fueled him as he punched Laughlin from behind, hitting him with a roundhouse blow to his right temple. Caught completely unaware, Laughlin's body jerked sideways, then tumbled to the floor.

"Oh my god!" Danny jumped up and gaped at the unmoving mercenary. Wide-eyed, he turned to Ryan. "Did you kill him?"

"No," Ryan said, moving around the couch. "Just knocked him out. With a punch my dad made me swear I'd never use. But it won't last long—we have to hurry."

Danny was dangerously close to losing it. "Please tell me you have a plan."

"Sure," Ryan said. "We grab Lawrence and Nadia and get out of here."

"Not quite as specific as I was hoping."

"Actually, I may have an idea." Ryan unclipped

the radio from Laughlin's belt. Making his voice as deep as possible, he produced a barely pass-able imitation of Laughlin's rough British accent and keyed the radio.

"Reilly, you still at the coach house?" he barked.

Danny's head dipped. "We're so dead."

But the radio squawked back immediately: "Right where you left us."

"Prisoners secure upstairs?"

"Yeah. Want us to load them up?"

"No, stay put." Ryan hooked the radio to his jeans, then snatched Laughlin's gun from the shoulder holster.

Danny stared at the gun. "What are you gonna do with *that*?"

"I don't know. But I definitely don't want him to have it."

"Just for the record—I hate this plan."

"I'm open to suggestions." Ryan ran to the double doors and looked out. The entry hall was empty.

Danny sighed. "Let's go get Lawrence and Nadia."

Ryan raced out, Danny hot on his heels.

CHAPTER
26

**LAKE TARU,
LOVANDA, AFRICA**

Crouching behind a low wall, Ryan studied the coach house. One of Laughlin's men remained at the top of the outdoor stairway, guarding the rooms where Ryan believed Lawrence and Nadia were being held. The other men talked and laughed inside the garage.

Danny squatted beside Ryan, his eyes squeezed shut as he muttered to himself.

"Ready?" Ryan whispered.

"Amen." Danny opened his eyes. "Haven't done that in a while. Let's hope it helps."

Ryan pointed the gun into the air. "Cover your ears."

He squeezed the trigger, the shot echoing across the compound. The guard on the stairs whirled around, weapon ready. Several men ran from the garage, alarmed. Recognizing Reilly among them, Ryan keyed his radio, imitating Laughlin's voice once more.

"Compound's under attack! Everyone to the front gates!"

"What about the prisoners?" Reilly responded.

"Leave 'em—everyone to the front!"

Reilly yelled for the other men to follow him. They grabbed their weapons and ran toward the entrance gates. The guard from the top of the stairs was the last to clear the area. When he was gone, Ryan leaped the half wall and headed for the rooms over the garage.

"Check the cars," he called back to Danny. "Find one with keys and start the engine."

Ryan acted on pure instinct. He couldn't afford any doubts right now. Moving quickly was crucial if he hoped to get them all out of here alive.

Taking the stairs two at a time, Ryan dashed to the second floor. The door was unlocked and opened onto a hallway that ran the length of the building. He flung open the first two doors, revealing an empty bedroom and bathroom. The next door was locked.

"Lawrence? Are you in there?!"

"Hello?" It was a woman's voice, hesitant and scared.

Ryan leaned in close. "Is that Nadia?"

"Yes—who are you?"

"I'm here to get you out." Ryan yanked on the knob, but the door wouldn't budge. He didn't have time to mess with it. "Back up all the way against the wall—hurry!"

Nadia confirmed she was out of the way as Ryan lifted Laughlin's gun. He hated guns but was glad he had one now. Ryan fired. The weapon jerked in his hands, the noise deafening in the confined space. But his aim was good and the lock blew apart. Wood splinters fell to the ground as Ryan shoved the door open.

Across the room, Nadia Cain glared at him from the corner. She held a piece of wood in her hands like a club. Ryan noticed the broken remains of a chair on the floor and realized she had fashioned her own weapon. Even frightened and exhausted, Nadia was still ready to fight her way out.

Ryan held up a hand, hoping to reassure her. "It's okay—I'm here to rescue you."

She couldn't hide her surprise. "How *old* are you?"

"Nadia!" Lawrence's panicked yell came from next door.

Ryan beckoned to Nadia to follow him, already moving down the hall. Any second now, Laughlin's men would realize they'd been tricked.

"Lawrence, it's Ryan—Declan Quinn's grandson!" Ryan leveled the gun at the door's lock. "I have Nadia. Back away from the door. We're getting you guys out of here!"

Ryan fired and the door flew open. Lawrence was still in the suit pants and shirt he'd been wearing when Ryan first met him, but they were now wrinkled and stained, the jacket and tie long gone. Dried blood from a blow to his head matted his hair.

Lawrence gaped, incredulous. "How did you get here?"

But Ryan just waved at him to hurry. "Come on! We have to run!"

Lawrence didn't hesitate, crossing the room quickly. As he came into the hall, Nadia ran into his arms.

"You're okay?" he asked, squeezing her tightly.

"Guys—we don't have time." Ryan raced for

the exit. Lawrence and Nadia followed, hand in hand.

Tearing down the stairs, Ryan was thankful to see Danny standing beside one of the SUVs with the doors open. From the direction of the main house, he heard the men yelling to one another in confusion. This was gonna be close.

As they approached the waiting SUV, Ryan looked back. "You can drive, right?"

Lawrence and Nadia traded a quick glance. "I'm better," Nadia said, moving to the driver's door.

"She's definitely better," Lawrence agreed.

Ryan pointed out the driveway that curved off to the private entrance. "Go that way. Get as far from here as you can."

As Nadia and Lawrence piled into the SUV, Danny realized Ryan wasn't coming with them. "What are you doing? We all have to go."

"I'll distract them, try to buy you guys some time."

"No, we stick together!"

Ryan pushed his friend into the backseat. "I'll get to the four-wheeler and catch up with you. Head toward the city!"

"Ryan—"

But Ryan slammed the door. Nadia looked at him through the window, unsure. "Go!" Ryan yelled.

She hit the gas, and the SUV lurched forward. As it sped toward the gate, Ryan moved to the three remaining vehicles. He aimed the gun at a tire and fired, blowing it out. Quickly, he shot the tires of the remaining vehicles, disabling them.

At the end of the long driveway, the SUV never slowed down. Nadia blasted through the gate, wrenching it from its hinges. The SUV screeched into a turn and sped off down the road.

Through the bushes, Ryan saw one of Laughlin's men returning. He dodged behind the garage structure just as the other man saw him. Bullets hit the side of the building as Ryan sprinted for the back gate.

Running hard, he fired the gun into the air a couple more times, then tossed it aside. If he created enough chaos, he might confuse Laughlin's men and be able to slip away unnoticed. Ryan cornered another building, then stopped short. One of the compound guards was coming at him, cutting off his escape.

"Kusimama!" the guard yelled, raising his rifle.

Ryan pivoted right, heading toward the rear of the chateau. A grand swimming pool with spraying fountains and a cascading waterfall blocked his way. He jumped over a chaise longue, skirting the edge of the pool.

From the opposite side, one of Laughlin's men appeared. "He's over here!"

Ryan dodged the other direction as the man gave chase. His access to the rear gate was now completely obstructed, ruining his chance for a quick getaway on the ATV. There was nowhere to turn but back toward the main house. French doors on the patio were propped open. He barreled through, praying he didn't run smack into Laughlin's guys.

Ryan entered a glass-walled sitting room. He took a moment to slam the French doors closed and lock them. With luck, the hired men wouldn't be anxious to shoot up Madame Buku's luxurious residence. He ran from the sitting room into the hallway, trying to get his bearings.

When he was halfway down the hall, another guard turned the corner in front of him. Moving too fast to stop, Ryan instinctively dropped into a power slide, slipping across the slick marble floor and plowing into the guard's legs. The unsuspecting man crashed to the ground, dropping his weapon.

Instantly, Ryan was up and on the move again. Shouts could now be heard all over the house. He was running out of time and options.

Ryan dashed through an arched opening and found himself back in the giant vestibule at the entry of the chateau. Through the gold-and-glass front doors, he saw Laughlin's men heading his way. There was nowhere to go but up.

As he reached the top of the stairs, Madame Buku suddenly stepped into his path. Ryan froze as two guards flanked her, rifles pointed at him.

Madame Buku examined him in surprise. "He's just a child!"

Desperate, Ryan turned back the way he'd come. But Reilly now blocked the bottom of the stairs. Then Laughlin himself pushed past his lieutenant, rubbing the side of his head where Ryan had hit him.

"Give me that," he growled, taking Reilly's gun. He climbed the steps toward Ryan. "I'm gonna teach this little sod a lesson."

"No." Madame Buku's tone was commanding. Ryan looked between them, caught in the middle.

"I wasn't asking permission." Laughlin took another step toward Ryan.

"The boy may prove useful." She waved a hand at her guards, and they started down the stairs. Ryan looked around for any possibility of escape. But there was nowhere left to run.

Laughlin reluctantly stood down as the guards grabbed Ryan from each side. Madame Buku stared at him with a predatory gaze.

"Besides," she purred. "There are punishments *much* worse than death."

CHAPTER
27

**LAKE TARU,
LOVANDA, AFRICA**

R yan had lost track of time. He believed he'd been sitting in the dark room with his hands bound to the chair for two or three hours, but he wasn't sure. When the guards left him there, he tried desperately to get loose. It was useless; the ropes were too tight. They chafed his wrists if he moved at all. Ryan kept expecting Laughlin to walk in and get his revenge.

But no one came.

The door was heavy and the walls were thick, so Ryan couldn't hear what was going on in the compound. With no windows and no light, he had nothing to focus on but his own chaotic thoughts. Did Danny, Nadia, and Lawrence get away? Had Kasey managed to get his messages to Mom and Dad?

Ryan tried some of the "games" his parents taught him over the years. Ways to distract his mind and stay calm. To focus on happier thoughts. But thinking of his parents just sent him into another spiral of worry and confusion.

His mind kept coming back to that photo album. The fact that he couldn't recall any pictures of himself as a newborn seemed odd. In all his parents' pictures he was already at least a year old. Even if some photos *had* been lost or destroyed, wouldn't someone have had a few? His grandfather? A friend of his parents? It didn't seem possible that there were no pictures of his mom pregnant or of him when he was born.

Unless, of course, they never existed.

Alone in the dark room with his questions and doubts, the most absurd and frightening possibility crossed Ryan's mind: What if Mom and Dad weren't his real parents?

He told himself he was being ridiculous. But the more he thought about it, the less absurd it seemed.

Ryan tried to focus on what he knew to be true. Mom and Dad were good people—the best.

They loved him and had even secretly trained him so he could be involved in the most private part of their lives one day.

So why not tell him the truth? Ryan's thoughts bounced around wildly, but kept coming back to one question: If he wasn't born Ryan Quinn, then who was he?

The door flew open, startling Ryan. A light flicked on, and he squinted, momentarily blinded by the sudden brightness. He could just make out the figure of Madame Buku glaring at him.

"Where are they?" she demanded. "Tell me where to find Anbo and Delilah, and I will let you go."

Ryan didn't respond. If Madame Buku was asking him where the others were, it meant they got away. If she had found them, he'd already be dead.

"Who are you?"

Ryan met her gaze. "Just a tourist. I got lost. Wandered into your compound by mistake."

Her faint smile was chilling. "Yes, that happens often. We find so many teenage white boys inside our walls."

"So if you'll just let me go . . . ?"

She ignored the comment, circling his chair. "I must admit, I'm fascinated. My men found no signs that anyone else helped you in your attack on my home."

"I didn't exactly attack."

"You're clearly a brave young man." Ryan wasn't sure how to respond to the unexpected compliment. She continued to circle, like a predator stalking its prey. "I think we're similar, you and I."

"We're nothing alike," Ryan said.

"I named my company Sekhmet after an Egyptian deity. Do you know of Sekhmet?" She sounded like a teacher.

"It's some kind of lion god."

"Very good. Sekhmet was a warrior goddess. A fierce hunter with a lion's head and a woman's body. For three thousand years, they say she protected the pharaohs and allowed them to rule a vast kingdom."

"Where they treated all the regular people as slaves?" Ryan couldn't resist the dig. Madame Buku carried herself like a queen. Her smug arrogance annoyed him.

"Society needs order. It's up to those who are strongest to provide it."

"All the people in that shantytown don't need *order*. They need help. They need food and a decent place to live."

Madame Buku seemed amused. "You know, you really should be more frightened of me." She stopped in front of him once more. "Do you know what I enjoy most about seeing someone so young with such courage?"

Ryan didn't say anything. He had a feeling he wasn't going to like the answer to her question.

She leaned in close. "It's such an effective lesson for the people when that fearless spirit is crushed. Broken. Destroyed."

Madame Buku crossed to the door, then looked back at Ryan. "I have eyes and ears everywhere. Even without your help, I'll find Anbo and Delilah—there's nowhere for them to run."

"They got away from you once. Maybe they'll do it again." Provoking her wasn't smart, but Ryan couldn't help himself.

Madame Buku's nostrils flared at the reminder of her earlier failure. "That will never happen! I'll watch them both hang in Liberty Plaza. And once I figure out exactly who you are, maybe you'll join them!"

Ryan didn't react, determined not to give her the satisfaction of seeing even a glimmer of fear. She took a breath, regaining her composure. Her unnatural calm returned.

"I have a feeling you're going to prove useful. Of course, I can't risk anyone finding you here. I'll have to hide you somewhere that no one will ever look." Madame Buku was enjoying herself again, toying with him. "Before I started Sekhmet Technologies, do you know how the Buku family made their fortune?"

"I bet it wasn't from anything nice."

"Gold. Our mine on Mount Satori was the first in Lovanda. Others came and went over the years, but only the Buku mine is still in operation today. The miners who work there call it *nyumba ya shetani*. The Devil's House." She opened the door. "Let's see how brave you are after you've spent a few days in the Devil's House."

Madame Buku walked out, shutting the door and leaving Ryan alone in the dark once more.

CHAPTER
28

**HOUDALI,
LOVANDA, AFRICA**

R yan might be dead, and it was all Danny's
fault. If he'd listened to the Quinns and
stayed out of the ERC's business, he
would've never found out about Madame Buku
and never jumped on that plane. Danny sat alone
in the corner of this no-frills apartment. He had
curled himself into a ball, knees to chest and
arms wrapped around his legs. From the street
below, the sound of cars honking and people
yelling wafted up to the third floor.

The last couple of hours had been tumultuous.
After Ryan forced him into the SUV and insisted
they go without him, Danny had demanded
Nadia stop and turn around. They couldn't leave
Ryan behind. But Nadia just drove like a demon

as Lawrence tried to calm Danny down.

"Your friend is smart. He'll get out," Lawrence assured him, but Danny could tell he wasn't very confident.

Nadia promised they'd find some way to help Ryan once they got to safety. But for the moment, there was nothing the three of them could do against a group of armed men.

Danny knew they were right, but he couldn't shake the feeling that he'd abandoned his best friend. He kept looking out the back window as the compound receded in the distance behind them.

Worried that Laughlin's team would soon be after them, Nadia turned off the main road. It had been several years since they'd lived here, but she and Lawrence still knew the area well. They took back roads until they finally arrived at the outskirts of Houdali.

During the drive, Lawrence and Nadia came up with a plan. They would contact their good friend Jaz. One of the only female rappers in Lovanda, Jaz knew every musician in the underground hip-hop scene and had helped organize their concerts. They could hide out with her to wait for Ryan and figure out what to do next. The problem was, they hadn't had any contact with people from their old lives for years. They weren't sure how easy Jaz would be to find.

The city of Houdali was loud and crowded. Narrow, twisting streets were lined with boxy apartment buildings in a general state of disrepair. As they drove, Lawrence and Nadia expressed surprise at the piles of uncollected trash on street corners and all the businesses now closed and boarded up. The city looked much worse than when they escaped. Only half listening, Danny stared out the window, numb, barely registering anything but his own fear.

Once they were inside the city, Lawrence had insisted they ditch the SUV and walk. Out on the streets, Danny was overwhelmed. All the things that should have felt exciting—the crowds of colorfully dressed locals, strange smells from steaming food carts, exotic music that drifted from sidewalk cafés—just seemed strange and scary. Danny stuck close to Nadia and Lawrence like a lost little kid.

After finally arriving at Jaz's building, they had a little luck. Jaz still lived in the same apartment and couldn't have been more excited to see them. She was a petite woman with beaded braids that hung down the length of her back. She pulled Lawrence and Nadia into her arms as tears ran down her cheeks.

Inside, Jaz had offered Danny something to eat. He shook his head, afraid that he was being rude, but not having the energy to care. In fact, he hadn't said a word to anyone since they'd arrived in the city. He retreated to a corner and slid down the wall.

Danny checked his phone. He was such an idiot—he'd forgotten to turn it off! He barely had any battery left. He needed to borrow a phone that had cell service and call the Quinns.

He looked over as Nadia sat next to him.

"Jaz knows some people who work for Madame Buku's company," Nadia said. "They're trying to find out what they can about Ryan."

Danny nodded, then looked away again. Nadia reached out and took his hand.

"I know what it's like. Feeling powerless, like there's nothing you can do. When I was four-teen, the police came to my house. The police in Lovanda are different than in America. Here, they are for sale to whoever pays them the most. They came to my house and took my father." Hearing the pain and anger in her voice broke through Danny's stupor. "They said he was a thief. My father worked for the city, and they accused him of stealing money from the city's bank accounts. It was all made up. My father would never steal."

"Why'd they do it?" Danny asked, pulled into her story.

"Because he told some friends he might run for the city council. He wanted to stop the corruption and decided to run against a man who had been the councilman for many years."

"So they just made up charges against him?"

"My father was a good man, but he was naive. They sentenced him to twenty-five years in prison. We weren't allowed to see him again."

Danny couldn't believe it. What kind of justice was possible if anyone could just buy off the cops?

"I'm sorry. That must be awful."

"My mother simply gave up. She became more like a ghost than a person. But I was always a fighter. A troublemaker, my father would joke. With no parent to talk sense to me, I was in trouble a lot. Stealing. Spray painting graffiti on government buildings."

"That doesn't sound too smart in Lovanda."

"It wasn't. I would have landed in jail eventually. And I was accomplishing nothing but hurting myself. But then I met Anbo." Danny followed her gaze across the room to where

Lawrence was speaking quietly with Jaz. "You should have seen him them. Strong. Full of ideas and opinions and passion. When Anbo spoke, everyone paid attention."

Danny found that hard to imagine, even though he'd seen the video of the concert. Sitting hunched over, there was little trace of the magnetic rapper left in Lawrence. He was all nerves and anxiety. That vibrant teenager was long gone.

"I wish I could have met him then."

"He was electric. Anbo believed that we all have something powerful deep inside if we can just find it. He showed me that I could use music and words to make a difference." Nadia smiled, remembering. "We were just teenagers. We had nothing. But once Anbo helped me find my voice, I never felt helpless again."

Danny imagined how great it would feel to have a talent like that. Where you could stand up in front of all those people and be heard. Where your own particular gift could actually make a difference.

Then he stopped. He'd been so worried about Ryan that he wasn't thinking straight. He *had* a gift he could use!

"Jaz," he called, standing abruptly. "Do you

have an internet connection?"

"Of course," she answered, showing him a beat-up old desktop computer. "But the internet in Lovanda is controlled by Sekhmet Technologies—you must be careful."

"Sekhmet won't be a problem. In fact, they're going to be my way in."

Danny sat at the computer. He opened a command window and began typing. The system was slow, but it would get the job done. When Danny first started hacking, he learned to always leave a backdoor into any network he visited, a secret way to get past security and firewalls in case he needed in again. It had become a habit for him and was the first thing he did once he got inside.

When he and Ryan got into Madame Buku's office computer, Danny had immediately opened a private web page where he kept the hacking programs he'd developed. Double-clicking on a program he named Mousehole had started the backdoor installation program. While Danny had composed the email to Kasey, the program downloaded. Madame Buku and Laughlin had interrupted them before he could send the email, but the backdoor should have completed the install on its own.

Danny finished typing his commands and hit enter. For several agonizing seconds he waited. Finally, a new screen opened that displayed the Sekhmet lion's head logo.

"What's that?" Nadia asked, looking over his shoulder.

"Madame Buku's desktop." Danny now had access to everything on her computer. He navigated to her email and opened it up. "There's some English and French, but what's this?"

"Swahili." Nadia quickly scanned the subject lines. "There, can you open that one?"

Danny opened it. "What does it say?"

"Something about a prisoner." Nadia read the email and frowned. "He's alive. Ryan's alive."

"Yes!" Danny cried, jumping up.

But the expression on Nadia's face didn't seem to reflect the good news. She looked to Lawrence, worried.

"He's being transported to Mount Satori," she said.

Lawrence deflated. "Then he's lost."

"What's Mount Satori?" Danny looked between them, but it was Jaz who answered.

"The mines. No one returns from the mines."

Danny wasn't about to accept that. "Well then, Ryan'll be the first. There has to be some way. We have to get him back!"

The three friends shared a look, and Danny could tell they thought it was hopeless. But he wasn't about to give up on Ryan.

Bang! Bang! The sudden knock on the apartment door startled them all. Had Laughlin's men found them? Or the police?

But then they heard a man's urgent voice. "Danny! Are you in there?"

Lawrence, Nadia, and Jaz looked his direction as Danny's face lit up with recognition. He raced to the front door and flung it open.

"Mr. Quinn!" Danny spontaneously hugged Ryan's dad, not even caring what anyone thought. "How'd you find me?"

"The GPS on your phone. Smart thinking leaving it on." As Danny pulled away, John scanned the room, taking in Lawrence, Nadia, and Jaz. Then his expression turned grim as he looked back at Danny.

"Where the hell's Ryan?"

CHAPTER
29

**MOUNT SATORI,
LOVANDA, AFRICA**

The road was chiseled into the side of the mountain. The SUV had traveled steadily uphill for almost an hour, taking the sharp curves fast enough to throw Ryan into the door repeatedly. Laughlin and the driver sat up front. Reilly was in back to keep an eye on Ryan.

Not that Reilly had much to worry about. Ryan was exhausted, having barely slept. His body ached from lying on the concrete floor with his hands bound for hours. He had finally dozed off when he felt Laughlin kick him awake. The men yanked Ryan to his feet just before dawn and tossed him into the SUV.

The rising sun crept over the ridge, casting long shadows across the mountain. From the narrow road up here, there was no view of the lake below or the countryside. Sheer cliffs of forbidding stone surrounded them on all sides. No wonder people called it the Devil's House.

The SUV pulled to a stop in front of a giant iron gate. A thick metal fence topped with razor wire made the entrance look more like a prison than a workplace. The gate opened and a guard with a submachine gun glanced at the driver, then waved them through.

Laughlin turned back and smiled at Ryan. "I think this is gonna be good for you, kid. Hard work builds character."

"Then I guess you've never done much," Ryan said.

"I'll give you this, you got backbone. Not that it'll do you much good here. In fact, it'll probably get you killed. These guys don't fool around."

Inside, a sheer cliff rose hundreds of feet straight up. At the bottom was a large tunnel opening that led into the pitch-black depths of the gold mine. Workers carrying equipment and baskets of debris lumbered in and out of the tunnel with the slow, sluggish pace of zombies.

The SUV came to a stop, and Laughlin turned once more. "We'll find your friends. The borders are sealed tight, and there's nowhere in Lovanda they can hide for long. Madame Buku has her nasty little heart set on making an example of them. And one way or another, Madame Buku always gets what she wants."

The back door opened, and Ryan was jerked out. Two men with guns slung over their shoulders yelled orders at him in Swahili as the SUV looped around and drove back out. The men pushed Ryan forward and he stumbled, barely righting himself before he fell.

The mining camp contained clusters of ramshackle buildings that had the feel of a military base. Some looked like offices and others more like barracks. Dump trucks and heavy machinery crisscrossed the area, engines rumbling and producing a cloud of dust. The whole place was dirty and loud.

The men marched Ryan over to a wiry little man whose left eye was white and cloudy. He examined Ryan with his one good eye, not bothering to hide his surprise.

"You very pale for Lovanda," he said in broken English. He looked to the two guards, and they all laughed. "I am foreman here. In charge. You work hard, no trouble."

Ryan tried to look as scared as possible. He wanted them to believe he was just a frightened kid who posed no threat. Appearing anxious wasn't that hard, since he was getting increasingly uneasy as he glanced around the camp. One side was blocked off by the metal fence and guards, the other by the steep mountain wall. Escape seemed next to impossible.

The foreman stepped close to Ryan, his voice dropping to a menacing whisper. "You are nobody here. No name. No family. Nothing. You do as told, that is all. Understand?"

This guy was just a bully, used to bossing everyone around. But Ryan couldn't afford to antagonize him, so he simply nodded. "I understand."

"Good." The man smiled again. "Then is time to work."

The foreman gave orders to the men in Swahili. One of them grabbed Ryan's arm and led him toward the mineshaft entrance. As they crossed the camp, Ryan saw that it was separated into three main areas. On the far side, a huge piece of machinery banged noisily as it crushed rocks and debris. Dump trucks came and went, watched closely by armed guards. The opposite side of the camp housed the long, wood buildings that Ryan guessed were barracks, and the center was comprised of metal trailers used as offices. Ryan noted power lines and a satellite dish atop one of them. Maybe a way to get a message out if he could sneak inside?

As they approached the front of the mine, Ryan was shocked to see several little kids. They were dirty, their clothes tattered. Seven or eight years old at the most. The kids carried buckets of water back and forth to a giant trough full of muddy sludge. Ryan felt the anger rise in him again—how could anyone do this to kids?

He was shoved from behind and kept walking. A group of men of all ages were gathered at the front of the mine. Everyone held a shovel or pickax, and some wore straps around their heads that held small lights. Even at the start of the day, they were all filthy and looked fatigued.

As Ryan approached, their eyes fastened on him in astonishment. They clearly weren't used to seeing anyone here who wasn't black. Everyone began whispering and pointing as a ripple of excitement spread among them.

The man in charge barked orders, and they responded instantly, going quiet and lifeless once more. As they began to trek into the tunnel, Ryan was nudged into line with them. A kid in front of him turned and studied Ryan for a moment, then seemed to come to a decision. He handed Ryan his shovel, then pulled a small axe from a belt around his waist.

"Stay close. Do what I say, okay?" The guy was probably seventeen, Ryan guessed, and his English was good. He glanced warily at the man in charge, and Ryan got the feeling the kid was taking a risk by helping him.

"Thanks," Ryan said.

They entered the tunnel, leaving daylight behind. Ryan took a deep breath, trying to calm his nerves, as he descended into the Devil's House.

CHAPTER
30

**HOUDALI,
LOVANDA, AFRICA**

Ryan's dad worked all night. Danny had struggled to stay awake and help, but had finally passed out and slept for several hours. *Nanay* always said he could sleep through anything. Guess she was right.

When he woke, the sun was already up. Mr. Quinn had taken over the kitchen table. It was covered with maps, photos, and information about Mount Satori and the mine. Danny yawned and stretched as he walked over. He still felt tired, but Ryan's dad looked as focused as he had the night before.

"Sorry I fell asleep," Danny said.

"Don't be. One of the first things you learn in the field is to eat and sleep whenever you can."

"And to use the bathroom," Danny added. "I figured that one out, too."

Mr. Quinn allowed a small smile, the first since he'd arrived, then turned back to a satellite image he was studying. Danny looked over his shoulder, seeing that he had circled an area in black ink.

"Did you find a way in?"

"Maybe." He pointed to a squiggly line that led away from the circled area. "This is an old access road. More of a dirt path, really. It leads around to the far side of the mining operation."

"You can hardly see it."

"Yeah. It's a hike in. Several hours, probably."

"And what do you do when you get there? How do you get to Ryan and get him out?"

Mr. Quinn frowned. "Still working on it. He could be anywhere inside the camp. I have to locate him, secure him, and make it back out. All without being detected."

Danny nodded, seeing the problem. "And you won't exactly blend in."

"No," he agreed.

"But I would." They both turned to see Lawrence behind them. He and Nadia had emerged from the back bedroom. In a T-shirt and jeans, Danny thought Lawrence looked less like a bank teller and more like a regular guy. "Nobody ever tries to break *into* Mount Satori. If you got me inside, I could find Ryan. I could bring him to you."

"It's too dangerous," Mr. Quinn said, but Danny could tell he didn't really mean it. He was just saying it to give Lawrence a way out.

But Lawrence didn't back down. "Your father saved us once. Your son saved us again. We owe your family this."

"Are you sure?"

Nadia stepped beside Lawrence, taking his hand. He looked at her, silently asking her permission, and she nodded. Lawrence looked back to John. "Tell me what to do."

Ryan's dad stood up, newly energized. "I actually have an idea. It's risky, but I think it's our best shot."

Danny was excited. "This is great! What can I do?"

"Sorry, Danny," he said. "You're going home."

"What? I can't go before we save Ryan." No way he was going to leave his friend behind again.

But Mr. Quinn was insistent. "You have to. I contacted a woman I trust in the ERC. She's picking you up here tonight and getting you out of the country. She'll make sure you get on a plane to New York."

"That's not fair! I can help."

Nadia offered encouragement. "You already helped. You're the one who found Ryan in the first place."

"The best way you can help is to do what I ask," Mr. Quinn added. "I need to know you're safe at home with your family. You got dragged into this because of us—"

"I did it myself. I'm the one who jumped on the plane."

"Danny, this isn't up for discussion." He reached into a duffel bag and pulled out a blue passport. "My first responsibility is to get you home safely. That's what I intend to do."

Danny took the passport and opened it. He recognized a photo of him taken for last year's school yearbook. But it had the name "Anthony Sedona" printed next to it.

This sucked. His first real *fake* passport and he couldn't even enjoy it!

CHAPTER
31

**MOUNT SATORI,
LOVANDA, AFRICA**

Ryan dumped another bucket of rocks and dirt into the metal cart. After several hours of hard work, his back was aching and his arms felt as limp as rubber bands. They had taken one short break for a few minutes, but that was more than an hour ago. Ryan was hungry, thirsty, and wiped out.

An air horn sounded through the mineshaft, and the boys and men began walking back toward the central cavern. Malik was the kid who had been quietly helping Ryan, explaining to him what to do and how to stay out of trouble.

"We eat now," Malik said. "Is very bad, but you must eat as much as you can. For strength."

Ryan nodded his agreement as they fell into line with the others. The gold mine was a confusing network of long, narrow shafts that veered out in several directions from the main tunnel. Lit only by strings of dim yellow lights, the shafts were dark and claustrophobic. Ryan had spent all morning collecting the rocks that Malik chipped away from the walls with his small axe. Some of the rocks held tiny flakes of gold. Malik explained that the heavy equipment outside would pulverize the stone into dust so the gold could be removed.

Everything about the mine felt primitive, like nothing here had changed for ages. The miners used handheld tools. Metal carts rode along rusting steel tracks. It was like an old Indiana Jones movie, only it was real. The entire operation depended on the cheap, backbreaking labor of the workers. Ryan wondered how long some of these guys had been down here. And how long they actually lasted in this gloomy environment.

The shaft opened into a large cavern. Everyone grabbed a bowl and lined up to get food being dished out of metal pots. When it was Ryan's turn, he stared into the pot and his stomach turned. It was a cold stew with unrecognizable vegetables in thick, brown goo. So gross.

"Told you." Malik was beside him. He grabbed the ladle and filled both their bowls. "No dessert, either."

They found a place to sit. The relief was instantaneous. Ryan didn't know how he was ever going to stand and walk again. He just wanted to curl up and go to sleep. He forced himself to take a bite of the disgusting lunch—it was as awful as it looked. He swallowed, then took another bite.

"How'd all these guys end up here?" Ryan asked Malik.

The teenager considered him with a guarded expression. "Bad choices or bad luck. Many of the men were arrested. Police say jails are too full. Send them here to work."

"Were you arrested?"

Malik shook his head. "No. I am here because of bad luck. My mother died. I had no one, so they send me here. All the young ones you see, they have no families. No one to miss them. No one to ask where they are."

"So they just get shipped off?"

"This is how it is in Lovanda." Malik stuffed

another bite into his mouth. "I think you have bad luck, too."

"Yeah. I seem to have a lot of it lately." Ryan finished the last bite of his stew, noticing how many stares he was getting. Some were simply curious, but others were hostile and suspicious. A group of bigger guys were looking in his direction and whispering to one another.

Malik noticed them, too, his expression darkening. "I am afraid more bad luck is coming."

Having moved to so many new places in his life, Ryan was used to being a stranger. He knew how it worked. Most kids just ignored you, maybe a few were friendly. And there were always losers who wanted to challenge you, to show how tough they were. But if he was going to find a way out of this place—and that's exactly what he planned to do—he needed allies, not enemies.

Glancing around, he had a sudden inspiration about how he might accomplish that.

After wolfing down their lunch, most of the workers were finding ways to relax. A few had closed their eyes to take a short nap. Some sat talking quietly. Others gathered in small groups using the rocks for makeshift mancala games.

But Ryan's attention was on a kid who was shuffling a deck of playing cards and preparing to deal.

Out of the corner of his eye, Ryan saw one of the bigger guys stand and move aggressively toward him. Ryan jumped up and went over to the kid with the cards. He squatted next to him, intentionally putting his back to the big guy.

"Sorry to bother you guys," Ryan said, putting on his friendliest smile. "Want to see something kind of cool?"

Clearly, none of them spoke English because they all just stared at him in confusion. Ryan pointed to the cards, then held up one finger, asking them to let him borrow them for one minute. He could feel the big guy looming behind him. Hesitantly, the kid handed over the deck. The cards were beat-up and torn, but they'd work fine.

With a flourish, Ryan shuffled the deck three times, faster than the eye could follow. Then he spread his hands apart and flicked the entire deck through the air card by card. They formed a blurry arc as they flipped from one hand to the other.

That got everyone's attention.

Since he was little, Ryan had practiced sleight

of hand with playing cards. He had become so adept, he could make it seem like the cards were practically dancing in his fingers. It was a form of meditation for him, keeping his body busy so his mind could roam free when he was puzzling over something. But the skill also came in handy in other ways.

Murmurs of appreciation went up from those watching as Ryan whipped the cards into a perfect fan, then closed the deck once more. He tossed it behind his back and over his shoulder, catching it effortlessly without looking. Using only the fingers of his right hand, Ryan separated the cards into groups, flipping them one over the other in a dizzying display that almost seemed to defy physics.

Quick as a flash, he reached out toward one of the kids and pretended to pull a card from his ear! Everyone's eyes went wide with surprise as they laughed. More workers moved over, wanting to see. Behind him, Ryan could sense that the big guy who'd been advancing on him was just as fascinated as the others.

For the next few minutes, Ryan performed every card trick he knew. He got claps and cheers as the crowd circled him. When the air horn finally sounded again, he squared the deck up and handed it back to the kid he'd borrowed it from.

"Thanks," he said.

Ryan felt a powerful hand hit him in the back. He turned to see the big guy right behind him. But he was grinning now. He slapped Ryan once more in approval, then headed off.

As everyone trudged back to work in the mineshafts, there was laughter and animated conversation. The workers didn't look at Ryan with suspicion anymore but with appreciation. Anyone who brought a little light to this miserable place was welcome.

Malik stepped past Ryan, picking up his axe once more. "I think maybe you know how to make your *own* luck."

Ryan was glad to have avoided a fight. But as he began scooping up another shovelful of rock, he knew it was going to take more than luck to get him out of here.

CHAPTER
32

**NEW YORK,
USA**

Kasey grabbed a yogurt and the orange juice from the refrigerator. It was a cold and gray morning, which perfectly matched her mood. She had planned on meeting her friends Emily and Janelle this afternoon to hang out, but really didn't feel like going. Winter break was usually a time to relax and have fun, but Kasey couldn't stop worrying about Ryan and Danny.

After getting home yesterday, she'd tried to learn as much as possible about Braxton Crisp. Not that there was much to find. The antique weapons dealer kept a low profile. There was a short profile about him on the store's website: Crisp was born in Massachusetts, was the son of a watchmaker, and had degrees from both Yale and Oxford. His shop had been in existence for just over ten years. Kasey searched for hours but couldn't find any more information about what he'd been doing between getting his degrees and starting his antique arms business. It was like Crisp just disappeared for nearly twenty years.

Jacqueline had been upset that Kasey went into the antiques shop on her own. She had clearly regretted her decision to let Kasey help. When they got back to the brownstone, Jacqueline insisted that Kasey go home.

"But I got Braxton Crisp's name," Kasey countered. "He never suspected a thing."

"And it may turn out to be an important break for us," Jacqueline said. "This has nothing to do with your abilities. I think you're an incredibly smart and resourceful young woman."

Kasey was surprised at how much Jacqueline's words meant to her. "Then let me stay."

"I'm sorry. I appreciate all you've done, but it has to stop now."

That had been the end of the discussion. Kasey tried to argue, but Jacqueline was unwavering. Kasey finally gave up and left. She felt strangely disappointed. Not just because she couldn't help the ERC, but because she enjoyed spending time with Jacqueline.

Kasey loved her dad deeply, but that didn't stop her from missing her mother. Mom passed away when Kasey was young, so Kasey mostly knew her from old photos and videos. Her father and brothers were great, but she often wondered what life would have been like if her mother had lived.

Spending time with Jacqueline felt a little like being with a mom. The hours they spent trailing Tasha had been awkward at first. But as time passed, they started talking. Not about anything important, just about school and the holidays. It had been nice, and Kasey was sorry to see it end.

"Did you finish all the orange juice?"

Kasey was surprised to see Drew at the refrigerator. She hadn't noticed him come into the kitchen. "Um, yeah, I guess."

"Then put it on the list." He closed the refrigerator and wrote "OJ" on the magnetized grocery list. Drew opened a bag of bagels, looking at her with concern. "What's wrong?"

"Nothing." Drew could be exasperating, but he somehow always knew when anything was bothering his little sister.

"Did Ryan do something?" His tone was instantly confrontational, ready to protect Kasey from the world.

"No. And Ryan and I are just friends, anyway."

"Right." He put the bagel into the toaster and pressed the handle down. "So what is it then?"

Kasey swirled the spoon around in her yogurt for a few seconds, then admitted, "I was just thinking about Mom."

Drew sat beside her at the breakfast table. "You remember much about her?"

"Not really. But sometimes I wonder what it'd be like with her still here."

"You definitely wouldn't be able to run around on your own as much as you do. Mom worried about everything. Dad's a lot more chill."

"Do you think we'd be totally different people if she was still here?"

Drew actually took a moment to consider before he responded. "Maybe not totally different. But a little, yeah. I think we are who we are *because* of what's happened to us. We wouldn't necessarily be better or worse. Just different."

That seemed exactly right to Kasey. Sometimes, people assumed Drew was dumb because he was a jock. Kasey thought he did it on purpose, not letting his friends see how smart he really was. At home, though, Drew was more himself and that was when she liked him best.

Her phone buzzed and Kasey glanced down, hoping it might be Jacqueline with some news. When she saw Danny's face on the Caller ID screen, she snatched it up and stood.

"I gotta take this."

Drew didn't miss a beat. "You gonna finish that orange juice?"

"All yours." Kasey hurried to her room, answering the call. "Danny?"

"Yeah, it's me—"

"Are you okay? Is Ryan with you? Where are you? Oh my god, what were you guys thinking!"

"Wow. And I thought *I* was stressed out." Danny's voice sounded like it was just around the corner, not halfway around the globe. "I'm fine, but Ryan's in trouble. His dad's on his way to try and rescue him."

"To rescue Ryan? But you guys were supposed to be rescuing Lawrence and Nadia."

"We did, but things got complicated. Listen, I managed to hack into the phone carrier here, but they can trace me if I stay on too long. I just wanted to make sure you knew Ryan's dad found us. He's making me take a plane home tonight."

"Where are you?"

Talking fast, he updated her on getting Lawrence and Nadia out of Madame Buku's compound and the backdoor he hacked into her computer network, which had revealed where Ryan was being held.

"Wait a second," Kasey interrupted, glancing down at the information she'd printed out about Braxton Crisp. "You hacked into Madame Buku's network?"

"It wasn't hard once we were inside her place."

Kasey's wheels were spinning. In her searches, she hadn't discovered any useful intelligence on Braxton Crisp. But one thing she did know is that he was greedy. Which gave her an idea, a way they could hurt Crisp where it mattered to him the most.

"Do you still have access to a computer?" she asked Danny.

"Yeah, until I leave for the airport."

"Good. I need you to do something for me."

CHAPTER
33

**MOUNT SATORI,
LOVANDA, AFRICA**

This was starting to feel like a terrible mistake. Volunteering to sneak into the mine had seemed like the only option back in the safety of Jaz's apartment. But out here in the dark, Lawrence was having serious doubts. He stayed close to John Quinn as they made their way up the overgrown path. But the closer they got, the more Lawrence felt the urge to turn and run.

The truth was, he had been running ever since leaving Lovanda. Lawrence had tried to settle into an ordinary life in America. He put on a suit he hated and a tie that choked him. But it never felt right. He was always uncomfortable, looking over his shoulder like someone was chasing him. Nervous. Fearful. He didn't even recognize the man he had become.

"Stop," John whispered. He knelt low, motioning Lawrence to do the same.

Up ahead, a ten-foot-tall chain-link fence topped with barbed wire surrounded the mine. A guard patrolled inside, casually checking the perimeter. Despite having a submachine gun slung over his shoulder, he looked bored. Lawrence held his breath until the man wandered back into the shadows.

"There." John pointed to an area where the fencing butted up against the mountainside. "I have bolt cutters to get through the chain link. You'll have to be careful of passing guards."

"Okay." Lawrence couldn't keep the tremor from his voice.

"I know you're scared. If you want to stop now, no one will blame you."

No one but myself, Lawrence thought. "I can do it. I have a much better shot at getting around unnoticed and finding Ryan than you."

"Then let's move while we have the chance."

John made a beeline for the spot. He wore a backpack, which he pulled off as he crouched beside the fence. Reaching inside, he produced bolt cutters. Working quietly and efficiently, he snipped sections of chain link to create an opening. When he was done, he replaced the bolt cutters in the pack and pulled out a thin tin can. The label on top read Salerno Sardines.

"No, thanks," Lawrence said, not hiding his distaste. "I'm not hungry."

"Good. 'Cause you don't want to eat these." John handed him the sardine tin, then held up a small remote control like the ones used to open car doors. "That tin is packed with plastic explosive. Just enough for a small explosion. Once you find Ryan, place this wherever it can cause the biggest distraction. This remote detonates it."

Lawrence took the remote nervously. "You're sure it won't accidentally go off?"

"It's perfectly safe until you trigger it. You have to hit all three buttons at one time to set off the charge. The moment you do, get back here as fast you can. I'll be waiting to get you both out."

Lawrence slipped the sardine can into his pocket. "All three buttons at once. Got it."

John put a hand on his shoulder. "You can do this."

Lawrence took a deep breath, gaining confidence from John's reassuring tone. Then he nodded—he was ready.

John pulled back the fencing, and Lawrence slipped inside. They had studied the satellite map images and chosen this side of the mine complex because there were a few buildings that housed equipment and machinery here. It would be empty at night.

Lawrence ran through the shadows, keeping close to the buildings. He leaned against walls and peered around corners, checking for guards. Dressed in shabby, dirty clothes, Lawrence would fit in once he found the workers. But if the guards spotted him now, they'd assume he was trying to escape and would shoot him.

Slowly, he made his way across the complex. He could see the brighter lights of the barracks area and used them as his guide. As he got closer, Lawrence heard voices and music. It sounded like the homemade instruments Lawrence played in his village growing up.

Lawrence was so distracted by the music that he almost walked right into the back of a guard. At the last moment, he saw the man a few feet ahead and froze. The guard was looking the other way, swaying back and forth. He seemed to be enjoying the music as well.

Backtracking carefully, Lawrence changed course and skirted around the outside edge of one of the barracks. The chattering of men and boys became more distinct. He followed the sound. Slipping between two of the buildings, he emerged into a huge courtyard filled with activity.

The barracks formed a ring around this common area. In the center, a large bonfire burned brightly as people talked, played games, and sang songs. Lawrence guessed there must be almost a hundred young men and boys here. It felt like a school at recess.

Lawrence was mesmerized for a moment. He'd expected everyone to appear broken and despondent. But somehow, they were finding moments of pleasure even in these horrible conditions. He felt an unexpected sense of pride in his countrymen.

He noticed one of the teenage boys staring at him. Lawrence turned his focus back to the mission. Moving into the crowd, he put his hands inside his pockets, reassuring himself that the tin of explosives and the remote were still there.

Weaving in and out of the assorted groups, Lawrence crossed the common area. As he passed the musicians, banging on homemade *djembe* drums and shaking their *shekeres*, he was reminded of countless nights making music with his friends. Glancing back, he discovered that the teenager who had stared at him was now following from a distance.

Lawrence tried to appear relaxed as he picked up his pace. There were so many faces. But no sign of Ryan. He turned and saw that two other young men had joined the teenager. They were shortening the distance, closing in.

Lawrence sidestepped through a group, trying to lose them. How had they figured out so quickly that he didn't belong here? After five years in America, did he really stick out that much?

He suddenly stopped, turning back to a small group he had just passed. Ryan's face was so caked with dirt and grime that Lawrence had almost missed him.

"Ryan!"

Ryan looked over in disbelief. "What are you doing here?"

"I'm with your dad. We're getting you out."

Instead of being excited, Ryan appeared concerned as he gazed over Lawrence's shoulder. Lawrence turned to find the guys on his tail were now right behind him. And there were more of them—at least ten, gathered in a pack. All staring at him.

Ryan stepped forward, tensing for a fight. But then the teenager who first followed Lawrence broke into a smile.

"I knew it—it *is* you!" He turned to the others. "Anbo! Anbo has returned!"

Before Lawrence knew what was happening, he was swarmed. These guys weren't threatening him. They were enthusiastic fans, cheering and clapping and welcoming him home.

CHAPTER 34

**MOUNT SATORI,
LOVANDA, AFRICA**

Ryan hung back at the edge of the crowd. As news of Anbo's arrival spread among the workers, almost everyone migrated over. Occasionally, he caught glimpses of Lawrence, lit by the flickering flames of the bonfire. He seemed overcome, unsure how to handle the reception he was getting.

Malik stepped up beside Ryan. "You are full of surprises."

"They really love him, don't they?" Ryan had noted the crowd's passionate reaction when he watched the video of Anbo and Delilah performing. Seeing their devotion up close was different. These young men viewed Lawrence as a long-lost hero returned.

"Anbo and Delilah were much more than singers. They gave us a voice. Their music helped us believe it might be possible for things in our country to change. I know all of their songs by heart—we all do." Malik watched Lawrence through the crowd. "I was fourteen when Anbo and Delilah were arrested. When they were sentenced to death, we were devastated. It felt like our government was killing a part of each of us."

Across the courtyard, Ryan saw a guard noting the large gathering, curious about what was going on. The man grabbed his radio and said something, his eyes on the crowd.

"Then a miracle happened," Malik continued. "They escaped. Somehow, they outsmarted the government. The rich might have all the power in Lovanda, but they could not destroy Anbo and Delilah."

Ryan felt a sudden surge of pride as he realized something. "My grandfather Declan was one of the people who rescued them. He got them out of the country."

"And now you have brought him back." Malik gave Ryan a warm smile. "Yes, full of surprises."

Ryan looked back at the guard as another joined him. They watched the crowd carefully, pulling rifles from their shoulders and holding them in a ready position. The crowd was drawing too much attention.

Leaving Malik, Ryan pushed his way through the throng. He finally made it to Lawrence. The young men and boys were asking him to sing. Just one song, they begged, offering up their suggestions. Their excitement was contagious, spreading through the group. But Lawrence remained frozen, overwhelmed and looking like he wanted to bolt.

"The guards are noticing," Ryan whispered to him. "We should get out of here while we can."

Lawrence's gaze darted to the edge of the courtyard where the guards gathered. His expression changed, becoming harder. The sight of the guards with their automatic weapons was making him angry. Ryan saw something shift inside Lawrence. His fear seemed to melt away. There was something different in his eyes now—a strength that Ryan had not seen before.

Then, surprisingly, Lawrence began to sing.

For a moment, the song couldn't be heard, drowned out by the voices of the crowd. But as those closest to Lawrence realized what was happening, a hush rippled through them. Lawrence's voice was hesitant and unsteady. He was singing in Swahili, a traditional song that was both haunting and beautiful. It sounded old, maybe something he'd learned growing up.

But as he continued, Lawrence's voice gained conviction. His tone became richer and his volume increased. The sound of a drum joined in. Ryan turned to see a boy moving forward, accompanying Lawrence.

Lawrence's uncertainty vanished as he began to move to the music. He sang to everyone around him, giving the distinct impression that he was performing for them alone. They leaned in, pressing closer.

The moment the traditional African song ended, Lawrence launched into a rap. He rapped in English, the words like staccato gunfire full of anger and betrayal. Ryan was amazed by the instantaneous transformation. The singer before him radiated charisma and confidence. No longer was he seeing Lawrence—this was Anbo:

Kept down low, no place to go,
No way to grow, to show what I can do—
Waking up, still in the dark.
Tossin', turnin', need a spark
To light my way.

Who am I? Just a man-child wanting
    more,
A wave can't make the shore,
Always reaching out, then pulled
    away . . .

Ryan was so transfixed that he didn't see Malik come up behind him.

"They're coming."

There were now four guards moving toward the crowd. Their fingers gripped the rifle triggers, ready to fire as they yelled at the workers.

Lawrence finished the rap and the crowd broke out in riotous cheering. Those farther back pushed closer, forcing Ryan aside. After shoving several guys out of the way, Ryan was finally able to grab Lawrence's elbow.

"We have to go—*now*."

Realizing the guards were closing in, Lawrence pulled himself away from everyone and followed. Malik pointed to the barracks on the far side.

"Go there. We will keep the guards away."

"Come with us," Ryan said, not wanting to leave him behind.

But Malik was insistent. "No. You take Anbo.

You must get him out of this place. Like your grandfather."

"I can help you, too."

"Go!" Malik grinned. "We will make a little luck for you."

Before Ryan could say thanks, Malik turned and shouted at the others. They responded immediately, forming a wall between the guards and Ryan and Lawrence.

Taking advantage of the opportunity, Ryan led Lawrence across the yard. They dashed between two of the buildings, not stopping until they were safely in the shadows beyond the barracks.

"You said my dad's with you?"

"Yeah, he's waiting for us at the fence," Lawrence said. "But he's all the way on the opposite side of the complex."

"The guards will be on high alert now."

Lawrence pulled the sardine tin from his pocket. "John gave me this. It's some kind of explosive. He said it's not that powerful, but it should be enough to distract the guards."

Ryan took the sardine can. His first thought was to set it off by the front gates so some of the people here could escape. He quickly dismissed that option. Even though a few might make it out, many would undoubtedly be shot.

How could he help Malik and the others without getting them killed?

Remembering his long day in the mine, Ryan was struck by an idea. He couldn't free everyone forced to work here. He just might, however, have a way to shut the entire operation down for a while.

But for his plan to work, he was gonna need a much bigger boom.

CHAPTER
35

**NEW YORK,
USA**

asha stormed down the sidewalk toward the antiques shop, furious at Braxton Crisp. She now realized she'd made a huge mistake getting involved with him. The man had no moral code whatsoever.

Crisp had promised never to sell the identities of anyone she or her father had helped during their ERC missions. It had been the most important demand Tasha had made when she'd agreed to work with him. But just this morning, she had received an emergency call alerting her that a woman they had rescued five years ago had been abducted last night.

Tasha was pulsing with anger, not just at

Crisp, but at the whole situation. It was John Quinn's fault she had betrayed the ERC! If he hadn't abandoned her father and left him to die alone, none of this would have happened.

She refused to let her father's legacy be destroyed. That obnoxious little toad Crisp had agreed not to sell those identities and she would hold him to it.

Tasha entered the antiques store, slamming the door shut and locking it behind her. She flipped over the sign in the window so it showed the shop was closed. Sitting at his desk, Braxton Crisp peered at Tasha over the rim of his reading glasses. He always looked supremely annoyed when she visited.

"Do we have an appointment?" Crisp disdainfully checked an open notebook on his desk. "No. We do not. And at present, I'm quite busy."

"Yeah, seems like you're swamped." The shop was completely empty. Tasha threw down a copy of the *Boston Globe* newspaper. "Front page news in Boston. An abduction."

"How tragic." Crisp didn't even glance at the newspaper.

"My father helped that woman settle there. You promised not to sell those identities—we had a deal!"

Crisp stood, picking up the paper. He looked ridiculous, Tasha thought, in his bow tie and old-man suit, surrounded by all these historic weapons. She felt like grabbing one of the Civil War swords off the wall and using it on him.

"You have my word, I had nothing to do with this." Crisp tossed the newspaper back at her.

Tasha instinctively caught it, realizing too late that it was a trick. Crisp had diverted her attention from his true intention. He lifted a device that looked like a gun except for its bright yellow color. When he pulled the trigger, two barbed electrodes shot out, hitting Tasha before she could move. The electrodes were attached to long thin wires.

Tasha's whole body jerked as the Taser zapped her with thousands of volts of electricity. Her muscles went rigid, pain shooting through her body. For a moment she convulsed and then dropped to the floor as the current finally subsided.

"Ms. Levi, I'm afraid your usefulness has come to an end." Crisp walked calmly around the desk and looked down at her. From his jacket pocket, he withdrew his cell phone and made a call. "I need you to dispose of some garbage. Enter from the back."

Tasha knew she had to fight or she was as good as dead. She struggled to move, but her muscles wouldn't obey. All she could do was look up helplessly as Crisp towered over her.

"Emotion makes you weak," he said. "It makes you reckless. Easy to manipulate. Your father really should have trained you better."

Inside her head, Tasha roared, wanting to make Crisp pay for those words. But she couldn't even lift a finger to stop him as he zapped her once more. This time, she nearly passed out.

Through a haze, she felt her wrists and ankles being duct-taped together. Another piece of tape was stretched across her mouth so she couldn't talk. Within minutes, a big man dressed in a tracksuit entered from the back of the shop. He lifted Tasha as if she weighed nothing and slung her over his shoulder.

As they exited into the alley, Tasha saw a sedan with its trunk open. She desperately tried to hit or kick Crisp's goon, knowing this might be her last chance. He barely even noticed. The big man tossed her in the trunk and slammed it closed.

Tasha slowly regained her wits. The trunk was pitch-black. She could barely move. She probed around, trying to find a jagged piece of metal or something she could use to tear the tape and get free. She was frustrated to realize that the trunk was completely empty. Obviously, this guy was careful, which would make it even harder for her to get away.

They drove for over thirty minutes. Tasha was certain they had left Manhattan as the traffic noise gradually diminished. The car bumped along, causing her to bounce from side to side. The cramped space was uncomfortable, and it was hard to breathe with the tape over her mouth.

Alone in the dark, she couldn't stop thinking about Crisp. He had said she was easily manipulated. But what did he mean exactly? Had he manipulated her in some way she didn't understand? Had Tasha been so determined to avenge her father's death that she let herself be duped by Crisp? She had a sick feeling in the pit of her stomach, and it wasn't just from her current situation.

The sudden squeal of brakes jolted Tasha from her reverie. The car slammed to a stop as the sound of crunching metal shattered the quiet. Tasha rolled into the back of the trunk, smashing her shoulder hard.

They had rear-ended another car. Tasha heard voices and the closing of car doors as the drivers got out. The words weren't clear, but the other driver was a woman who sounded upset and angry.

This might be her chance. She had to get the woman's attention. Tasha turned on her back and tried kicking the trunk lid. It was awkward—she didn't have much room, so the kicks weren't very powerful. But she managed to make a little noise. Beneath her duct-tape gag, she let loose with a muffled scream.

The voices suddenly stopped. Tasha wanted to yell at the woman to run and get help, but couldn't even move her lips. She kicked the trunk lid again.

Then Tasha recognized the sound of somebody getting punched. And again. A body hit the side of the car and fell to the ground outside.

Defeated, Tasha quit kicking. Crisp's thug had knocked the woman out, maybe even killed her. Her last chance had failed.

Keys rattled in the trunk's lock, and the lid suddenly opened. Bright sunlight blinded

Tasha. She blinked rapidly as a silhouetted figure loomed over her.

But it wasn't Crisp's muscle. It was the woman.

"Hello, Tasha," Jacqueline Quinn said. "We need to talk."

CHAPTER
36

**MOUNT SATORI,
LOVANDA, AFRICA**

T he diesel fuel cans were stacked across from where the dump trucks were parked for the night. Ryan checked the first two, disappointed to find them empty, before picking up one that was half-full.

"Take this," he said, handing it to Lawrence.

"We have to hurry." Lawrence peered around the end of one of the trucks, keeping watch for guards.

"I know." Ryan found two more cans that still held some fuel. He didn't actually want much liquid. Explosions were caused by the diesel vapors—the gases trapped inside the can—not by the fuel itself. Three should be plenty for what he had in mind.

"Come on," he whispered.

With a can in each hand, Ryan snuck across the complex, using the equipment and machinery to keep out of sight. Lawrence followed, less fearful and more confident since his impromptu performance. Finally, they made it to Ryan's target.

The stone crusher was a huge metal monstrosity, old and battered with a giant drum sitting on a raised platform two stories up. A network of conveyor belts carried chunks of stone up to the mouth of the beast where they were pulverized and the gold extracted. Ryan set his diesel cans down and climbed the scaffolding to the raised platform.

"Pass them up."

"What is this?" Lawrence asked as he handed the cans to Ryan.

"This baby crushes all the stone. Without it, the mine comes to a standstill."

Ryan tucked two of the cans under the main drum and the other right next to the crusher's motor. He pulled out the sardine tin filled with plastic explosive and positioned it halfway between the two points. If this worked right, one small explosion would now become several big ones. At this time of night, no people were in this area, so the only damage would be to the machinery.

Ryan jumped down from the platform. "Once we get closer to my dad, we'll trigger it."

Keeping to the shadows, they retraced their path around the barracks. The uproar in the courtyard seemed to have calmed down, but there were still a lot of guards in the area. Lawrence took the lead, guiding them around the buildings and back toward the hole in the fence.

"It's that way." Lawrence pointed, but Ryan couldn't see very far in the dark. "We're close."

Ryan heard a soft crackling sound behind them and spun around. He couldn't see anyone, but that had sounded like static from a walkie-talkie. Then the hum of an engine approaching became unmistakable.

Behind them, a guard emerged from the corner of the building, his rifle raised. Ryan grabbed Lawrence's shirt and yanked him around the corner as a shot rang out. The bullet hit the edge of the metal structure barely missing them.

Lawrence and Ryan dashed along the side of the building. A truck suddenly appeared, cutting them off. Ryan turned back, but the guard was now blocking their retreat.

The wiry foreman with the cloudy eye got out of the passenger side of the truck. He pointed at Ryan and Lawrence, yelling commands to his men in their language. They closed in, leaving nowhere to run.

Ryan's hand slipped into his pocket, grasping the remote control. All three buttons at once, Lawrence had said. Ryan's fingers found each of them. The guard behind him was now very close as Ryan pressed the buttons, praying this worked.

Ka-boom! A ball of fire blasted into the sky as a thunderous explosion rocked the mine complex. The foreman and his men all looked up in shock and confusion.

Ryan didn't hesitate, whirling and grabbing the guard's rifle. He whipped it out of the startled man's grip, then hit him with a Krav Maga Straight Punch right in the chin. The guard fell to the ground, but Ryan was already turning.

A second explosion shook the ground as he charged the two men in the truck. Holding the rifle at each end, Ryan aimed at the driver who was raising a handgun. Ryan slammed into the man, using the rifle like a battering ram. The driver was knocked into the truck, hitting his head against the metal and crumpling to the ground.

Ryan turned toward the foreman, but he was too late. The man's face was twisted in fury as he punched Ryan in the side. He snatched the rifle out of Ryan's hands, then swung the butt end at him. Ryan blocked the blow with his arm. Pain shot through his shoulder as he fell to his knees. The foreman raised the rifle high overhead, prepared to deal a crippling blow.

But then he slumped over, tumbling to the ground. Lawrence stood behind him, a rock in his hand. His strike had knocked the foreman out cold.

"Let's go—the other guard's getting up!" Lawrence dropped the rock and grabbed Ryan's hand, helping him stand.

On the far side of the complex, the flickering glow of orange flames lit the night sky. The moans of wrenching metal reverberated through the camp as the stone crusher fell to pieces. Ryan thought it would take them weeks to get the mine running again. It wasn't freedom, but hopefully it bought a little reprieve for Malik and the other miners.

Still reeling from the blow to his side, Ryan hobbled after Lawrence. It hurt to move, but they had to reach the fence. As they passed the farthest building, a figure materialized from the darkness.

"Dad!" Ryan raced up to his father, never happier to see him. They hugged and then his dad pulled away, examining him with concern.

"Are you hurt?"

"Winded, but I'll be fine."

John glanced in the direction of the raging fire at the stone crusher. "What did you do?"

"Created a distraction." Ryan couldn't help grinning. "Maybe a little bigger than you originally planned."

Dad smiled at him with admiration. "Come on, we need to get out of here before they pull themselves together."

He led the way toward the hole in the fence, holding back the chain link as Lawrence ducked through. Ryan followed, grateful to leave the Devil's House far behind.

CHAPTER
37

**HOUDALI,
LOVANDA, AFRICA**

Danny checked the side mirror again. It was impossible to tell if anyone was following them, though. Even at night, the narrow streets of Houdali were packed with cars and trucks jockeying for position. At this rate, they'd never make it to the airport.

Danny glanced at Candace, the woman driving. Her eyes darted from side to side, checking for signs of trouble. Candace was Mr. Quinn's friend from the ERC. She was Ethiopian and no taller than Danny, but she seemed tough and experienced. She'd been very cautious when she picked him up from Jaz's apartment. They snuck out the back just in case the building was being watched. Security was getting tighter all over the city as the police searched for Anbo and Delilah. Candace had the car radio tuned to a news station, but Danny couldn't understand a word of what they were reporting.

He hated to leave without knowing if Ryan was okay. But Mr. Quinn needed his sole focus to be on helping his son. He couldn't afford to be worrying about Danny, too. This time, Danny knew he had to do as he was told, whether he liked it or not.

Fortunately, he'd been able to help Kasey before Candace showed up. Kasey's idea had been pretty brilliant. She'd asked Danny to go back into Madame Buku's computer network and see if he could access her banking records. They knew that Madame Buku had paid Braxton Crisp for Lawrence and Nadia's new identities. If they could learn the account number where she sent the payment, they might gain some leverage over Crisp.

It hadn't taken long to find it. Two weeks ago, Madame Buku paid two million dollars to an account at a bank in the Cayman Islands. The Caymans were where people put money they wanted to keep secret. There was no name to identify the owner of the account, just a number. But Danny was sure it was Crisp's.

Two million dollars! This scumbag was making a fortune selling people out. He sent the name of the bank and the account number to Kasey just before Candace arrived to pick him up. Hopefully, Kasey and Mrs. Quinn could somehow use it to help stop Crisp.

"Danny, get down."

Candace's tone was sharp. Danny did exactly what she said. He slid down in the passenger seat so his head was below the dashboard.

"What's wrong?"

"It's a road block." Candace kept her eyes forward the whole time she talked to him, not looking down. "They're checking every vehicle."

"You don't think my fake passport will fool them?"

"It should, John's work is always excellent. But it looks like the police have photos. They're checking every passenger. Is there a chance that any surveillance cameras might have seen you?"

Danny thought about Madame Buku's compound. Even though he never saw her face-to-face, she had security cameras around. Which meant she could have his picture.

"Probably," he admitted.

"Then we can't risk it." Candace inched the

car forward. Flashing blue lights now lit the interior. "I need you to open your door and slip out. There was a corner market two blocks back. If I'm not there in thirty minutes, you need to find your way back to the apartment. Can you do that?"

"Yeah. I can use the map on my phone." Danny had used Mr. Quinn's charger, so his phone was now at full power.

"Go quickly. Before they move this way."

Keeping his head low, Danny opened the passenger door. He crawled out, squeezing through so he didn't have to open the door very wide. He was in the middle of the street. Three vehicles ahead, he saw a police officer holding up a photo and inspecting the occupants of a truck. Danny scrambled to the back of the car and hid behind the trunk so he wasn't visible.

When the cars moved forward again, he zipped across traffic to the sidewalk and moved off in the opposite direction. He forced himself to stroll casually so he didn't attract attention. In less than five minutes, he was at the corner market.

Ten minutes passed. Then twenty. Thirty. And still no sign of Candace.

But Danny didn't freak out.

He checked the map on his phone and fig-ured out how to get back to Jaz's apartment. Sure, he was alone in a strange city in a foreign land. He didn't speak the language. And the cops were probably passing his photo around. But he felt strangely calm. He could do this.

The streets of Houdali were twisty and con-fusing. He got lost twice, but managed to figure out where he went wrong and head in the right direction. Staying in crowds seemed like the best way to go unnoticed, so Danny kept his eyes lowered and blended in as much as pos-sible.

Candace had been right—cops were every-where. Any time he saw one up ahead, he turned and took a different path. It took a while, but eventually he made it back to Jaz's street.

Danny was feeling pretty proud of himself as he turned the corner onto her block. But his good mood evaporated when he saw two squad cars with flashing lights parked in front of the apartment building. A group of people had gathered, their attention on the front door.

The door burst open, and a brutish cop came out. He pushed the onlookers out of the way. Using harsh language, he yelled at them to back off. Two more officers came out, escorting a prisoner.

Danny froze as he recognized Jaz. The young woman who had risked so much for her friends was defiant, struggling against them and forcing the officers to drag her away. They stuffed her into the back of a squad car as Danny waited anxiously.

Was Nadia coming out next? Did they get her, too?

But no one else emerged. The cops jumped in their vehicles and sped away with a screech of tires. Within seconds, the small crowd dispersed, upset and whispering among themselves.

Danny ran down the street and into the building. He took the stairs two at a time. The door to the apartment was standing wide-open. He rushed in, alarmed to see the place in disarray, furniture toppled over and things broken on the floor.

"Nadia?"

There was no one in the living and kitchen areas. The bedroom and the bathroom were both empty, too. The cops had searched the entire apartment. So what had happened to Nadia?

Danny heard the crunch of someone step-ping on broken glass out in the living room. He picked up a wooden tribal statue that had been knocked to the ground, holding it like a club. Stepping softly, he made his way out of the bedroom and down the hall. He breathed a sigh of relief, though, when he saw Nadia.

"There you are!" Danny said.

Nadia gasped, spinning around in shock, which quickly turned to confusion. "Danny? What are you doing here? You're supposed to be on a plane."

"They're locking the city down. The police are looking everywhere for you."

"They must be checking all of our old friends' places. We were lucky Jaz saw them arriving. She sent me to hide on the roof until they left." Nadia took in the trashed apartment, fearing the worst. "Where is she?"

"The cops took her. They didn't hurt her, though. Not that I could see."

Nadia's whole body sagged. "They will."

Danny had read and seen videos about people getting taken away by corrupt police in far-off countries. But he'd never known anyone personally who it happened to. Jaz had opened their home to them. Risked everything to keep their group safe. And now she'd been dragged off in the middle of the night. What would they do to her?

All of a sudden, those stories about people risking their lives for freedom in distant lands felt way too real.

CHAPTER
38

**NEW YORK,
USA**

asey had called Jacqueline twice since Danny sent the banking information on Braxton Crisp, but got no answer. She didn't want to risk saying too much in a voice mail, so she'd just asked Jacqueline to call back as soon as possible.

It was midafternoon in New York, the skies overcast again. Christmas was almost here, but Kasey wasn't feeling the holiday spirit. Not when there was so much to worry about. In a couple of hours, her two oldest brothers would be arriving home from college, and the whole family was going out for dinner. But for now, Kasey was on her own.

She decided to swing by the Quinns'

brownstone to make sure Jacqueline wasn't there. From the front, the place seemed empty. She knocked and waited, but no one answered. Kasey was about to leave when she noticed a blur of movement across the basement windows that looked down into the study. Was someone in there?

A metal rail at ground level kept Kasey from getting near enough to the windows to look inside. She leaned as close as she could and thought she heard voices—when a hand grabbed the back of her neck!

"Looking for something?" a man's deep voice growled.

Kasey turned, but the man held her in a firm grip. He was big, taller than Drew, with high cheekbones and long, black hair pulled back into a ponytail. She thought he looked Native American. His dark brown eyes glared down at her.

"I'm a friend of the people who live here," Kasey stammered. "I wasn't, like, trying to break in or anything."

The man studied her a moment more, then released her. He blocked the stairs up to the front door. "You should go."

"It's actually kind of important—"

"You should go now." The guy was built like a stone wall and wasn't budging.

Kasey realized he was keeping an eye on the brownstone—that's why he'd spotted her. He must be working with Jacqueline, which meant he was probably involved in the ERC. How could she make sure without giving anything away, though? Kasey suddenly had an idea.

"I have to talk to Jacqueline right away," she said. "I'm a friend of Varian Fry." Varian Fry was the journalist who had founded the original Emergency Rescue Committee, way back in World War II. Not many people would recognize his name.

But the large man in front of her definitely did. His brow furrowed as he studied her. "Jacqueline's busy."

"She needs to hear this." Kasey leaned in close, whispering. "It's about the leak."

That finally seemed to convince him. He stared at her a beat longer, then nodded toward the front door. "Downstairs."

Kasey hurried up the stairs and opened the door. She looked back to say thanks, but he was already moving away, positioning himself to keep watch on the brownstone. Kasey stepped in, closing the door quietly behind her.

Heated voices came from the study. Descending the staircase, she could make out Jacqueline's French accent.

"You betrayed us all. People have died because of you."

"Crisp had recordings. I heard Quinn admit that he abandoned my father!" Making it to the bottom, Kasey could see into the study. Jacqueline stood in front of Tasha, who was duct-taped to a chair but still defiant. "Quinn left him to die."

"No, he didn't. John went back for Isaac—even after I begged him not to. It was a suicide mission, but John wouldn't listen."

"You're lying," Tasha said, but she sounded uncertain. The two women were so focused on each other that they didn't notice Kasey just outside the door.

Jacqueline grabbed Tasha's chin, forcing the younger woman to look up at her. "Did you know that Braxton Crisp was a spy for twenty years before he went into business for himself? He's spent his whole career manipulating and controlling people. I don't know what this recording was that he played for you, but I can guarantee you it had been doctored. It certainly didn't tell the whole story."

Jacqueline was fierce. She let go of Tasha, then continued. "John and Isaac went into Iran to get that family out. What John told you was true, up to a point. Your father stayed behind to buy time. It was *his* choice. His priority was helping the family escape."

Kasey saw a change in Tasha's attitude. Jacqueline's words were getting through. Tasha knew she was telling her the truth.

"Isaac was wounded, but managed to hold off the members of the Republican Guard who were following them. John got the family to a boat on the Caspian Sea. That's when he called me. He told me he was going back to get Isaac."

"So why didn't he?"

Jacqueline's tone shifted, becoming gentler. "He did. But when John got back, he discovered the Republican Guard had captured Isaac. They tried to make him talk, but he refused. They had . . . hurt him. And then they killed him. If you don't think John still blames himself for not getting there earlier and saving Isaac, you don't know my husband at all. John didn't tell you the whole truth because he didn't want you to think of your father suffering. He hoped to spare you that, at least."

Tasha hung her head. Kasey thought she saw a tear roll down her cheek. "He tricked me. Crisp totally played me."

"The information you gave to him," Jacqueline said, back to business, "how did you know all the new identities? You weren't even involved in most of those rescues."

"Quinn gave them to us," Tasha admitted reluctantly.

"John?" Jacqueline was confused. "What are you talking about?"

"When we left Andakar, I brought Quinn to Crisp. He drugged him. Quinn gave us almost every person the ERC has rescued for years. And he doesn't remember any of it."

"Oh my god." Jacqueline stepped back, shocked.

"But maybe we can get them back. I know where Crisp keeps the list." Kasey thought Tasha sounded desperate. "He wrote all the names and the new identities in a leather journal. He keeps it locked up in a safe in his shop. We could get it back."

Jacqueline was still reeling. "He must have copies."

"I don't think so. Crisp is old-school—he

doesn't keep any digital files. He's too worried about being hacked. He's afraid of someone getting their hands on the names and selling them for themselves. He guards that journal like it's Fort Knox." Tasha leaned forward, unable to move much because of the restraints. "Please, let me try. I can make this right."

"You can *never* make this right," Jacqueline snapped. "Besides, how would we even get to it?"

"I may have a way." Kasey stepped into the room as both women turned in surprise. "Crisp loves money more than anything. So why don't we hit him where it hurts?"

CHAPTER
39

**MOUNT SATORI,
LOVANDA, AFRICA**

They had been trekking down the mountain for almost two hours. Ryan was already fatigued from the day's work in the mine even before they escaped, but he forced himself to ignore the exhaustion and keep moving forward. Lit only by the stars, the path they followed was steep and treacherous. But Dad had successfully led them safely away from the guards' pursuit.

This lower section of Mount Satori was dense forest. A chorus of buzzing insects and exotic birdcalls surrounded them. From the shadows, predators tracked their progress, calculating whether the trio might make a tasty dinner. The only animal brave enough to consider it was a leopard they'd crossed paths with earlier. But Dad's vicious growl and the beam of a flashlight in the big cat's eyes had sent it scampering off.

"We'll stop here." Dad motioned to an outcropping where two boulders were wedged together forming a crude cave. He took off his backpack, dropping it to the ground. "We've got blankets, food, and water in the pack. You two set up here, I'm gonna do a quick recon."

It was strange seeing his father like this. Ryan had done plenty of camping trips with Dad, but he was completely different now. More like a soldier, constantly vigilant and alert for trouble. This was the side of him that was the ERC operative, a side Ryan had never seen in action before.

"We're staying here?" Ryan asked.

"Until first light. Lawrence and I hid a car at the base of the mountain, less than an hour away. It'll be safer to travel in the morning when there's traffic on the roads. We'll drive back into Houdali, get Nadia, and get the hell out of Lovanda."

"You should take your son to safety first," Lawrence said. "Delilah and I will only make it more dangerous for you."

Dad glanced at Ryan, then back to Lawrence. "We're *all* getting out. I'll be back shortly."

A moment later, he disappeared into the shadows. Ryan and Lawrence ducked into the cave and opened the pack, both of them hungry and thirsty. As he leaned back against the rock, Ryan's feet tingled with relief. He felt like he could sleep for hours.

He looked at Lawrence, realizing something. "You called her Delilah just then. The only time I've heard you do that was when we first watched the video of her singing."

Lawrence sat back now, too. "Since we left, she has been Nadia. It was safer to think of her that way—to forget about Anbo and Delilah."

"Must be a lot harder to do now that you're home."

"To be honest, it was never easy. I tried to hide. To be someone else. I thought I could leave all this behind. But being back here, seeing the suffering—this is where we were always needed." Lawrence took a long drink of water. "Delilah was always more of a fighter than I was. I remember telling her that our voices were our weapons, our way to fight back. She never forgot that. But I did."

Ryan understood what he meant. "The

reaction those guys at the mine had as they watched you was amazing. You're a hero to them, even after all this time."

"I guess the music lived on, even if Anbo and Delilah didn't."

Ryan leaned his head back, closing his eyes for a moment. He was so tired. He felt like it had only been a few seconds when a loud shriek woke him.

Ryan bolted up, surprised to discover the sun was shining. It was morning—he must have slept several hours.

"It was just a bird," Dad said, looking down at him. "An egret, I think."

Ryan sat up, rubbing his eyes. Lawrence was nestled in the corner, still asleep on the hard ground. Ryan looked at his father, sitting at the mouth of their little cave.

"Did you sleep at all?" he asked.

"There'll be time when we're on our way home." Dad was nonchalant, but Ryan could see the dark circles under his eyes. "I put some cream on your hands. They were pretty scraped up."

Ryan looked at the scratches and cuts from working in the mine. The white residue from the lotion was still visible. He realized they didn't sting like they had last night and felt a sudden, overwhelming sense of gratitude that his father was here.

"Thanks." Ryan scooted closer, so their talking wouldn't wake Lawrence. "Danny must be almost home now."

Dad checked his watch. "Should be. I can't get a signal out here, but I'll check in and make sure as soon as we get down."

"You must be pretty mad at us."

"Actually, no. I was worried, but not mad."

"Really?"

"The truth is, I was helping Granddad on ERC rescues when I was younger than you. Don't tell Mom I told you that—I promised I wouldn't encourage you."

Ryan smiled. "She wants you to be a hypocrite, huh?"

"Absolutely. Being a hypocrite's part of being a parent. You'll find out one day." Dad handed Ryan an energy bar. "But I was the same when I was your age. If I saw something that needed doing, I'd just jump right in. Didn't really think about the danger or the consequences. I'm afraid it's the Quinn curse. It's in the blood."

Ryan took a bite of the bar. He chewed slowly, thinking back to that night in the brownstone looking at the family photo album.

It seemed like ages ago, but it had only been a few days. Finally, he swallowed and looked up at his father.

"Why are there no baby pictures of me?"

Dad's head swiveled quickly, meeting Ryan's gaze. Several emotions flickered across his face: surprise, sorrow, resignation. "That's a long story."

Ryan's stomach clenched. His father wasn't denying anything or making excuses. "I'd like to hear it."

"Are you sure?"

Only now did Ryan realize how much he'd been hoping he was wrong. But there was no turning back. He needed to know the truth.

"I wasn't born Ryan Quinn, was I?"

"There's something I want you to know first." Dad reached out and took his hand. "You're the best thing that ever happened to Mom and me. You're the love of our lives, and we'd do anything for you. You're our son in every way possible."

Ryan said nothing. He couldn't. He just waited for his father to continue.

"But the name you were born with is Kostya Balazar . . ."

PART*THREE*

CRANK UP THE VOLUME

CHAPTER
40

**LORAND,
PELSKOVA**

TWELVE YEARS AGO . . .

The timing had to be perfect.

John Quinn checked his watch. Seven minutes until the operation went live. He was unusually nervous today because of the baby. Rescues involving children were particularly complicated and dangerous. Often, the ERC refused to even take on those cases. Too many things could go wrong.

But Ludo Milankovic had begged Declan and John to help this young woman and her son escape. Her name was Nina Balazar, and Milankovic had been a close friend of her family since she was born. He believed she'd be killed if they didn't get her out of Pelskova soon.

"There she is."

Jacqueline's voice snapped John's attention back to the mission. Jacqueline was looking at a young woman pushing a baby stroller through the busy crowd. Nina wore a heavy green coat and a furry winter hat. Ten feet behind, two uniformed soldiers shadowed her every step.

The guards were part of an elite unit that protected Janos Balazar and his family. Balazar was the iron-fisted dictator of Pelskova, a harsh and ruthless ruler. He was also Nina's father-in-law and the grandfather of her child. A few weeks ago, Balazar's son had died unexpectedly. Nina was heartbroken at losing her husband, but also scared to now be living without his protection inside the presidential palace. Immediately after the funeral, Balazar ordered his guards to start following Nina and his grandson everywhere.

Balazar suspected that Nina was secretly working with revolutionaries inside Pelskova to bring him down. The moment he had proof, he planned to order Nina's execution and take his grandson, Kostya, to raise as his own. Which meant this mission had to be a success, because the tyrant was right. Nina had been helping the rebels and eventually the truth would come out.

There would be no second chances for Nina and her baby.

Jacqueline and John tracked Nina's progress, following her from the next aisle over. Once a week, the central square of Lorand transformed into a sprawling outdoor market. Farmers brought in eggs, dairy products, and whatever vegetables and fruits they could grow in this cold Eastern European climate. The market was huge, surrounded on all sides by imposing government structures built back when Pelskova was a Soviet republic. It was also one of the only places Nina was allowed to visit outside the presidential compound.

Nina moved slowly, taking her time as she inspected merchandise at various stalls. Occasionally, she paused, leaning down to check on her baby and to wrap his blankets more tightly.

"She's following the instructions perfectly," John said.

"We make the switch when she turns into the next row." Jacqueline pulled out a furry hat exactly like the one Nina wore. She was already wearing a wig and a green coat that made her a near-perfect match to Nina.

John looked to Jacqueline. "Ready?"

"Always."

They made a great team. John worried about Jacqueline because he loved her, but he never doubted her abilities. She had been working with the ERC for a couple of years and was a natural. John had thought he might never settle down with anyone. What woman would accept how uncertain and dangerous his life was? But Jacqueline was proving the exception.

He might even propose to her soon if he could work up the nerve.

"We're on." Jacqueline straightened the hat and stepped forward, John right behind.

As Nina turned the corner at the end of the aisle, she was out of the guards' view for a few seconds. Moving with synchronized efficiency, Jacqueline and John swept up next to her. Jacqueline swapped places with Nina as John scooped up baby Kostya, replacing him with a child's doll.

"Back this way," John whispered. Holding the baby against him, he steered Nina behind the nearest stall.

The switch was completed in an instant. By the time the guards turned the corner, Jacqueline was pushing the baby stroller, and John had pulled Nina out of sight. From the back, Jacqueline could easily pass for the young mother. She led the guards away, casually saun-tering down the long aisle.

"We have to move fast," John said. Nina was scared but holding it together. John handed her a gray coat and a wig. As she changed, he checked on the baby in his arms.

Kostya had big eyes and curly hair. He was grinning, as if this was all great fun. John couldn't help but smile as he gazed down at the boy.

"How do I look?" With the new hair and coat, Nina appeared quite different.

"Perfect. Hold my hand—we're just a normal couple. We have to be fast, but casual. We don't want to draw attention."

John led Nina through the crowd, keeping Kostya pressed tight to his chest for warmth. "Hopefully, this will give us at least a twenty-minute head start."

"I don't know how I can thank you all."

"Let's just worry about getting you out of here, okay?"

No one gave them a second look as they passed out of the market and onto the city streets. A block away, John had parked an old Audi sedan. He strapped Kostya into a baby seat, then started up the car and sped away. The streets were narrow and claustrophobic, lined with apartment buildings in states of disrepair. As always, John had the route memorized.

Taking Nina and the baby from the market had been the only option, but it had an inherent challenge. The city of Lorand was bordered by a mountain on one side and dense forest on two others. That left only one direction in and out of town. If they didn't get past the city limits before the alarm was raised, they'd be trapped.

"We may have a problem." Jacqueline's voice crackled through the communicator earpiece John wore. "There's another soldier walking toward me."

John pressed the talk button. "Abort. Now."

"You haven't had enough time—"

"Get out, Jacqueline! Meet at the extraction point. Understood?"

"Understood," she said, frustrated.

John hit the gas, taking the corner with a squeal of tires. Jacqueline would turn off the main aisle now, discarding the coat and wig to change her appearance. With luck, she'd make it out of the market and to the motorcycle they'd hidden and be on her way within minutes.

"We're not going to make it, are we?" Nina asked.

"We're gonna try. Hang on." John powered

through a few more turns, checking his mirrors for signs of a tail.

As they approached the next intersection, John heard sirens approaching. Rounding the corner, he was forced to hit the brakes. Already, vehicles were stopping as police blocked off the boulevards leading out of the city. He slammed the gearshift into reverse. But behind them, cars blocked the way. They were wedged in, unable to move forward or backward.

Nina saw that they were trapped. "If Janos gets Kostya, he'll turn him into a monster like himself. I can't let that happen to my son. You must hide him."

"We're not done yet." John searched for a way out, but didn't see any options.

Nina looked back at Kostya, tears in her eyes. She kissed her fingertips, then touched the baby's feet. *"Ja velmi chabe kachayu. Da spatkanya."*

"We'll make a run for it," John insisted. "We can hide out in the city."

But Nina was resolute. "Promise you'll get him somewhere safe. Somewhere he can grow up happy. Janos will never stop looking for him. Whatever it takes, I beg you, keep my son away from him."

"Nina, we can still—"

Before John could say anything more, she swung the car door open and jumped out.

"Nina—no!"

But she was already gone, running toward the police cars blocking the road. John watched in horror as she waved her arms and yelled at them. Nina looked around frantically, then raced across the street and into a park. Within seconds, the squad cars took off after her, sirens wailing.

The blocked vehicles began to move once more. John was torn, watching helplessly as Nina disappeared into the park's trees pursued by police. From the backseat, Kostya began to cry. John looked back at the boy, his heart breaking.

"I know, buddy. I'm so sorry." John put the Audi in gear and pressed the gas, then made the turn that would lead them out of the city, to safety.

CHAPTER
41

**MOUNT SATORI,
LOVANDA, AFRICA**

A mile outside of Lorand, a helicopter was waiting to fly us across the border and into Lithuania," John finished. "Jacqueline—*Mom*—was already there when you and I arrived. We waited for Nina as long as we could."

"But the police caught her?" Ryan asked. He was numb. Overwhelmed. Trying to process that all this wasn't just a story Dad was telling him. It had really happened. To *him*.

"Nina knew they would. Your mother sacrificed her life to ensure your safety. It was the most courageous thing I've ever seen." John leaned his head back against the cave wall. "For the next few weeks, Mom and I took care of you while we tried to figure out what to do. Granddad called in every favor he could to try and rescue Nina. But a month later, Balazar announced to the world that she had died. An illness, he said, that took both mother and baby."

"He killed her." Ryan's stomach twisted into a knot.

"We're not exactly sure what happened. But Ludo Milankovic knew someone on the inside. They got word to Nina that you were safe. Whatever happened, she knew you were okay."

"Ludo Milankovic—that's *Principal* Milankovic, right? He knew Nina?"

"Their families were close. She was like a younger sister to him. It's why we chose that school for you when we settled down in New York. We knew he'd always keep an eye on you."

"When he said he wanted me to know the truth, that's what he meant. He wanted me to know about Nina."

"And I'm glad you do." Dad's expression darkened. "But we still have to be careful, Ryan. Nina was right—Janos Balazar has never stopped looking for his lost grandson. It's why Mom and I kept it from you."

On the other side of the cave, Lawrence yawned and sat up. He rubbed his eyes, blinking at the morning light. "Guess they didn't find us," he said.

"No, and hopefully they think we're long gone by now." John stood. "We should get down to the car and back to the city. We need to get out of Lovanda as soon as possible."

They quickly stashed the blankets and supplies into the pack. John slung it on his back, checking to make sure the coast was clear.

Ryan was struck by a thought. "How come you and Mom decided to keep me instead of setting me up with a family?"

"You stole both our hearts. It just seemed right."

"You weren't even married yet."

Dad grinned sheepishly. "Only because I didn't have the guts to ask. Sneaking into countries where you could get shot on sight is nerve-racking. But it's a piece of cake compared to proposing."

CHAPTER
42

**HOUDALI,
LOVANDA, AFRICA**

In daylight, the trek down the mountain was easy. They found the car where Dad and Lawrence left it, still hidden and undisturbed. The roads were busier now, and they blended into the traffic heading toward Houdali.

In the backseat, Ryan stared out the window. Dad's story had turned his whole world upside down. It would take a while to sort out his feelings. Mostly, he kept thinking about how brave his birth mother had been. Nina had allowed herself to be taken prisoner so her son could be free. He wondered if he looked like her. And what about his birth father—he still didn't know anything about him. What had it been like being the son of a tyrant?

So many questions.

Part of him was mad at Mom and Dad for not telling him about all this before. It was his life; he had a right to know. But the truth was, they had done what Nina asked. They'd kept him safe all these years. They'd loved him, protected him, even taught him the skills he would need to survive if the truth was ever discovered.

Ryan was the only living heir of a brutal dictator, but he was also the great-grandson of one of the founders of the ERC, a group that had saved thousands of people around the world.

So what was he—a Balazar or a Quinn?

"We need to ditch the car," Dad said. Ryan looked out the front window. Up ahead, police blockades were erected. Uniformed officers were checking all the vehicles entering and exiting the city.

"Take the next turn and park." Lawrence pointed up ahead. "I know how to get around the checkpoints. We had to do it often."

A few minutes later, they left the car and continued on foot. Lawrence guided them through a series of alleys and less-traveled streets. Ryan noticed his father frown at his cell phone.

"What's wrong?"

"I've got a signal, but no message from the

woman who was getting Danny to the airport."

"Can't you just call her?"

"I tried. Twice. It went straight to voice mail." He slipped the phone back in his pocket. "I'm sure it's fine."

But Ryan could tell he was worried.

"Something's going on," Lawrence said as they passed an open-air café. Inside, people were packed together watching an old television. On the screen, a reporter stood in front of a courthouse.

". . . the emergency trial is still in session behind closed doors. All five defendants have been arrested on charges of high treason, a crime punishable by death."

Lawrence couldn't hide his alarm. "Nadia . . ."

He turned abruptly and started running down the street. Ryan was about to follow, but Dad grabbed his shoulder.

"Walk. You and I stand out more here. We can't draw attention to ourselves."

It took all the willpower Ryan had not to take off after Lawrence. They walked fast, keeping their heads down as much as possible. But no one even noticed—everyone was huddled inside restaurants and shops watching the unfolding drama on TV.

After another two blocks, Dad opened the door to an apartment building, and they hurried upstairs. Ryan stepped inside the apartment and was immediately assaulted.

"Dude!" Danny wrapped his arms around him, then pulled back. "I totally thought you were a goner!"

"You always know just what to say," Ryan teased. "Why are you still here?"

Dad closed the apartment door. "Just what I was going to ask. What happened to Candace?"

"I don't know. The cops were stopping everybody. She made me get out of the car before they got to us."

John immediately pulled his phone out and stepped away. Ryan glanced across the living room, relieved to see Lawrence holding Nadia. They were both staring at a small television.

"We were worried. There was something on the news about a trial. We thought it might be for Nadia."

"It almost was. She was hiding on the roof. But they got Jaz, Ryan. I watched them drag her away."

Ryan stepped to the television as Lawrence looked up. "They've arrested our friends. People they suspect might be helping us."

Nadia turned up the volume. "They're bringing them out."

An officious man in a gray suit addressed the cameras and the crowd. "The highest court in the Republic of Lovanda has issued its ruling. All five defendants have been found guilty of high treason."

Nadia gasped. Lawrence held her tight, his expression furious. The camera panned along the five defendants as they were led out of the courtroom in cuffs. Jaz kept her head held high, but the fear in her eyes was unmistakable.

"The punishment for treason is death," the officious man continued. "The executions will take place at sundown tonight in Liberty Plaza."

Danny couldn't believe it. "That's impossible—there's no way they had a trial that fast."

"There's got to be some way to stop this," Ryan said, turning to Lawrence.

"The government appoints the lawyers for defendants. And treason is considered a crime against the nation. There are no appeals, and the sentence is carried out immediately. This is how justice works in Lovanda."

"We have to do something." Danny turned

to Ryan, but he was still focused on the screen.

"Look," Ryan said, pointing. "It's Madame Buku."

Looking regal in her designer glasses and colorful headwear, Madame Buku addressed the reporters. "I'm just pleased that Sekhmet Technologies was able to help gather the data that brought these conspirators to justice. When we learned that Anbo and Delilah had returned to Lovanda with the intent of launching terrorist attacks, we knew it was our duty to stop them."

"She's such a liar!" Danny was beside himself.

Madame Buku looked right at the camera now. "Of course, if Anbo and Delilah were as righteous as they claim to be, they would step forward and take the blame themselves. Instead, they allow their colleagues to go to the gallows in their place. Like all traitors, they are cowards."

"She's trying to bait you," Ryan said. "To draw you out."

"Well, it worked. We won't let our friends die in our place." Lawrence looked at Nadia, who wore a fierce expression.

"It's time to stop running," she said.

Danny turned the TV off. "No way. You can't

just turn yourselves in. That's exactly what she wants."

"She's left us no other option," Lawrence said.

"Maybe she has." Ryan turned to face them, an idea forming. "This Liberty Plaza where the executions are supposed to happen—is it a big public place?"

Nadia nodded. "The largest in Houdali."

"And there'll be a crowd there?"

"Of course."

Ryan looked at Lawrence and Nadia. "You told me the music you two made was your way to fight back. So let's fight."

Danny smiled. "You have that I've-got-a-plan look."

Before Ryan could respond, his father walked back into the room, hanging up from a call. "Okay, I think I have us a way out of here, but we need to move quickly."

They all shared a glance before Ryan said, "We can't leave yet."

"Yeah, we can. And we are. Let's go."

Lawrence shook his head. "We have to help our friends. We won't just abandon them."

"Dad, they're gonna execute five innocent people if we don't do something."

"And what exactly do you think we can do?"

"Rescue them."

"Come on, Ryan. How are we supposed to do that?"

"By working together. Isn't that what the ERC does?"

"ERC missions take time and planning and resources. What makes you think we can pull something like that off in a few hours?"

"Because we're Quinns. That's what we do."

His father was about to argue, but stopped, recognizing the determination in his son's eyes. He looked around at the others. They were equally resolute. Finally, he shook his head in resignation.

"Mom's gonna kill me."

That was all the permission Ryan needed. It was time to get to work.

CHAPTER
43

**HOUDALI,
LOVANDA, AFRICA**

Less than two hours to sundown, and there was still a lot to do.

The apartment had been turned into a command center. With everyone's help, Ryan's spark of an idea was transforming into an actual plan.

Lawrence and Nadia tapped back into the network of contacts that helped them stage their pop-up concerts five years ago. The response was immediate and enthusiastic. Their friends would do anything necessary to help stop the executions. Two women had arrived with outfits and makeup for Nadia. Several guys provided portable sound equipment and speakers. The teenage sister of one of them had rounded up two higher-quality laptops for Danny to use.

In the back bedroom, Ryan checked on Nadia and Lawrence. The two women were busy braiding Nadia's hair, weaving in strips of colorful cloth that matched the vibrant aqua-and-gold African gown they'd brought. As they worked, the rapper and hip-hop singer practiced lyrics to songs they hadn't performed in years.

"We have to go soon," Ryan said. "You guys need anything?"

Lawrence paced restlessly, unable to hide his anxiety. "How about another two weeks to rehearse?"

"You've got an hour." Ryan offered a reassuring smile. "You're gonna be great."

"That's what I keep telling him." Nadia took Lawrence's hand and squeezed.

Ryan headed back down the hallway. Framed photos lined the wall. Most of them were of Jaz surrounded by friends and family. Her bright smile lit up every picture. The thought of this warm, vibrant woman being used by Madame Buku to get to Lawrence and Nadia made Ryan livid. He continued into the living area, more determined than ever to free Jaz and the others.

At the breakfast table, Danny pivoted between Jaz's old computer and the two newer

laptops. They were all running different programs, complicated coding that Ryan couldn't
understand at all.

"You get into the systems okay?"

"Dude, we're in *everywhere*." Danny's eyes
had a feverish glaze, darting from one screen to
the next. His fingers clicked over the keyboards
like he was playing a concerto. "This is gonna
be epic."

"Ryan!"

Ryan glanced at one of the laptops, surprised
to see Kasey in a videochat window. "Hey!
What're you doing?"

"Danny's helping us stop the leak in the ERC."

"Us?"

"Your mom and me."

Ryan couldn't believe it. "Mom's actually letting you help?"

"Yeah." Kasey glanced away, then back, lowering her voice. "At least, I hope so. Technically,
we're still negotiating."

Ryan wasn't at all sure Kasey would win that
battle. "So who was the leak?"

Kasey hesitated. "Um, it's a long story. I'll tell
you when you get home. Your mom's here. You
want to talk to her?"

Ryan was about to say yes, but he glanced

across the room at his father. Surrounded by photos and maps, Dad was fine-tuning the plan and making arrangements. Ryan didn't know if he'd told Mom about the rescue. And he really didn't want to have to lie to her.

"Better not," he told Kasey. "We're pretty busy."

"We've got work to do, people," Danny said. "Just blow each other a kiss and say good-bye."

Ryan glared at Danny, but he didn't even notice, his gaze glued to a screen.

"See you soon," Kasey said. "Be careful, okay?"

"You, too."

Ryan crossed to his father, who was just hanging up from a call. "Everyone's almost ready."

"Good." Dad set the phone down. "That was Candace. She was detained by the police over-night, but they let her go."

"Was she hurt?"

"She's fine. I told her to get out of Lovanda, but she wants to help." Dad pointed to a circle on the city map. "This is Liberty Plaza. The con-cert will be over here at the park. A couple of miles away."

"Will Nadia and Lawrence be safe?"

"For as long as it takes the police to fig-ure out where they are and to get there." Dad looked up at him, serious. "Our success depends on whether the police respond the way we hope they will. If they don't, we have to terminate the rescue immediately."

That would mean leaving those people behind. Ryan couldn't imagine doing all this and not being able to save them.

Dad stood. "Listen, what's happening here—these people working together, trying to help—this is what the ERC is all about. We don't always succeed, though. And I won't lie, it hurts every time we fail. I remember the failures more than all the successes put together. But you have to be willing to walk away when necessary. Can you do that?"

"I guess."

"Not good enough. I have to know I can count on you to do what I say. You need to trust me."

"I do." Ryan didn't like it, but he knew Dad was probably right. "Whatever you say goes."

"Then sit down and listen up. We'll only get one chance to do this right."

CHAPTER
44

**HOUDALI,
LOVANDA, AFRICA**

By the time the sun dipped below the horizon, everyone was in position. They each had a vital role to play. As Ryan scanned the crowd at Liberty Plaza, he was filled with sudden misgivings. There were hundreds of people here. Police were visible everywhere. It was impossible to predict what might really happen once they set the plan in motion.

Forcing himself to set his fears aside, Ryan worked his way closer to the far end of the square. A platform had been constructed, high enough for everyone to see the gallows where the executions would take place. From a sturdy wood beam, five nooses dangled ominously, waiting for the prisoners. Officers with machine guns stood guard.

Ryan guessed there were several hundred people jammed into the plaza. They weren't excited or bloodthirsty, though. Instead, there was a subdued quality of nervous anticipation. Many appeared reluctant to be here, which didn't surprise Ryan. On the streets, police were rounding up citizens and forcing them to attend. Madame Buku was determined to create a spectacle.

Ryan spotted her on the balcony of a building that looked down on Liberty Plaza. Madame Buku had a view of everything from up there. Even from this distance, it was easy to see she was enjoying herself. She talked with Laughlin, who stood at her side. The British mercenary smiled at something she said, then glanced into the crowd. It felt like he was looking right at Ryan. Lowering his head, Ryan continued toward the gallows.

As the sun finally set, bright lights illuminated the square. Giant television monitors had been erected all around Liberty Plaza. Sekhmet Technologies would broadcast the executions throughout the entire country for everyone to witness. Of course, if everything went according to plan, they'd be getting a very different show from the one they expected.

"Police bus is pulling up now," a man's voice said through Ryan's radio transmitter. "North side, behind the stage."

Ryan veered that direction as his dad responded. "Copy. En route."

Ryan tapped his earpiece. "Almost there."

Two of Lawrence's friends, Caden and Lacey, were helping Ryan and his father. Caden's wife and Lacey's brother were both among the five prisoners, and they insisted on taking part. Dad had been hesitant about exposing them to danger. But the truth was, this rescue attempt wouldn't be possible without them.

"Good citizens of Lovanda," a voice bellowed. The same self-important man in the gray suit from the TV news report was now addressing the crowd. His pinched features appeared huge on the monitors all around the square. "As Minister of Justice, it is my responsibility to carry out the sentences decreed by the court."

As the man droned on, Ryan hurried to get into position. The success of the rescue would depend on timing. Right now, everyone's attention was on either the platform or one of the massive screens, which made slipping through the crowd easier. Ryan passed the gallows and made his way to the unlit darkness behind the platform.

The street back here had been closed. Only official vehicles were allowed through the blockade. Hiding behind a large planter, Ryan spotted the beat-up prison bus. It had to be at least forty or fifty years old, a metal rust bucket with bars across the windows.

A line of officers made sure no one got close as the prisoners emerged. All five looked haggard, their hands cuffed and ankles shackled as they shuffled along. Ryan recognized Jaz from the pictures in her apartment. But the warm smile he'd admired in the photos was gone. Like the others, she seemed dazed and terrified.

Ryan keyed his radio. "Prisoners are off the bus."

As the prisoners were led toward the gallows, the line of police officers dispersed. Dad had expected the bus to be all but forgotten once the prisoners were removed. He was right.

Within a couple of minutes, the only person left was the driver. He sauntered around to the front, casually lighting a cigarette and leaning against the hood.

Keeping to the shadows, Ryan slipped behind the bus. The Minister of Justice was now reading the prisoners' names and death sentences. They were running out of time.

Dad's voice crackled in his ear. "Everybody ready?"

"Ready," Ryan said.

Caden and Lacey both checked in: All set.

And then Danny's voice came through. "So ready!"

"All right then," Dad said. *"Go."*

In midsentence, the Minister of Justice was cut off, replaced by Lawrence's booming voice echoing through the plaza.

"Brothers and sisters, this is not justice!" A murmur of shock and excitement swept through the crowd as the video image of Anbo and Delilah filled every screen around the square. "We won't stand quietly in the dark any longer—we must be heard! No one dies today!"

As recognition dawned, a roar erupted from the crowd. Music exploded from the speakers,

CHAPTER
45

**HOUDALI,
LOVANDA, AFRICA**

Danny had been calling in favors all day. He hadn't realized how many friends he'd made in the hacker community over the past few years. Since it was mostly anonymous, he didn't really keep track of everyone he helped out or offered advice. But today, Danny was the one who needed assistance, and he couldn't believe the response he was getting.

Danny had used his backdoor into Madame Buku's network to gain access to Sekhmet Technologies. A brilliant hacker known only as P8riot showed him how to hijack the live feeds being broadcast from Liberty Plaza. Instead of airing the execution, Madame Buku's own company was now streaming Anbo and Delilah's surprise performance to the whole country. Sekhmet's security team was already working to block the hackers' access and regain control.

Danny had lots of chat windows open, allowing him to communicate with hackers around the world who were helping him keep the security team at bay. The concert feed needed to stay live long enough for Ryan and his dad to free the prisoners.

As Danny typed, he rocked out to Anbo and Delilah. The concert played through an open window, and it was hard to keep his eyes off the screen. They were singing in a park in front of a bronze statue of an African warrior holding a baby in his arms. They had managed to gather a guerrilla music crew, complete with portable sound system and colored lights. It looked very cool.

Using message apps and social media, Danny had spread word of the pop-up concert. There were over two hundred people there, with more arriving every minute. Fans held their cell phones high, recording and live streaming the performance.

Nadia looked fantastic in her Delilah persona. Her long braids whipped back and forth as she strutted in front of the statue. The colorful, traditional gown she wore made her look like she could be the bronze African warrior's wife. And her voice was beautiful—piercing and ethereal, like she was some kind of avenging angel.

Lawrence was just as intense. Dressed in ripped jeans and a T-shirt that read "Live Free or Die Tryin'," he seemed like a totally different person. He growled his raps, swaggering with pride and strength. The crowd went crazy for him.

Anbo and Delilah were back where they belonged.

Several of their friends were recording the concert, and Danny switched between the various cell phone feeds. He had to make sure the statue of the African warrior was clearly visible. That was the landmark that would let the police know where they were performing. If the cops didn't come for Anbo and Delilah, then the rest of the plan wouldn't work.

"Danny, we have to be out the door in ten minutes."

Candace had come up behind Danny without him even noticing. He had been happy to see that she was all right. Once again, she was in charge of getting him out of Houdali. Hopefully, this time it would go a little smoother.

"I need as long as possible. If I leave, the feed's gonna crash."

"Ten minutes," she said. "We're cutting it too close as it is."

Danny was about to argue for more time, but a video chat request chimed in. He accepted, and Kasey appeared in the window.

"We're all set to go," she said.

"Now?" Danny was already popping between so many screens he couldn't keep count.

"As soon as Jacqueline gives the okay." Kasey's brow creased. "You're ready, right? Our whole plan depends on you."

"Sure," Danny said. "Ready when you are."

He slid his chair to the second laptop and opened the program he'd use to take down Braxton Crisp. He didn't even have time to wipe the sweat that was dripping down his forehead.

Going back to being just a sidekick was starting to look pretty good.

CHAPTER
46

**NEW YORK,
USA**

C risp is there," Kasey said, staring at the antiques shop across the street. "I saw him move past the window."

Kasey and Tasha had a good vantage point from inside an Indian restaurant. Tasha had ordered chicken curry and two sodas, but only so they could take a table near the front window. Neither of them had an appetite. In fact, the fragrant smell of yellow curry was making Kasey a little queasy.

Tasha had barely spoken to her. The young woman's rage was unmistakable. One fist clenched her cell phone so hard the knuckles were white. Kasey pushed the plate toward her.

"Want some?"

"No." Tasha didn't even glance at it. Her gaze was locked on Braxton Crisp's shop. Kasey wasn't very fond of Tasha, but she understood the pain she had gone through.

"I lost a parent, too," she said. "Nothing hurts that much."

Tasha turned, fire in her eyes. Kasey had the feeling she was about to tell her to go to hell. But something shifted. For the first time, Kasey saw a crack in Tasha's tough facade. She stared at Kasey a moment, then nodded slightly.

"No. Nothing does."

"It helps to talk about it. I had my brothers and my dad. Do you have anybody you can talk to?"

The defensive armor was back in an instant. "I don't need anybody."

"Yeah? How's that working out for you?"

Tasha clearly didn't like being told what to do, especially by a teenager. But Kasey had been through it herself and knew she was right.

Before Tasha could respond, Jacqueline's voice crackled through the walkie-talkie on the table between them. "We're in position."

Tasha hit the talk button. "Crisp is inside. We have visual confirmation."

"Kasey, is Danny ready?"

Tasha raised the walkie, and Kasey leaned in. "As soon as you give the word."

"Then tell him to do it. Tasha, make the call, then watch the front."

"Got it."

Kasey felt a thrill of excitement as the operation swung into action. Braxton Crisp kept the leather journal where he'd written down all the ERC identities locked tightly away in his safe. Their goal was to trick the horrible little man into removing it so they could steal it from him.

Kasey's role was supersmall—all she had to do was call Danny. Jacqueline didn't want her getting close to Crisp again. But at least she was getting to do *something*.

Kasey hit the video chat app on her phone. Within seconds, she was connected to Danny again.

"If we're gonna do this, it has to be now," he said. "Mr. Quinn's friend is about to drag me out the door."

"We're good to go. You sure it'll work?"

"When that douche bag looks at his bank account again, he's gonna need new underwear!" Danny turned from the screen, typing on another computer. "All right, the program's running. Gotta go."

"Danny, you're the best."

"Have to admit, hearing that never gets old." He winked and the video chat cut off.

Kasey gave Tasha a thumbs-up. Tasha dialed, leaning in a little so Kasey could hear. After a couple of rings, Kasey could just make out Crisp's voice as he answered.

"Braxton Crisp. How may I be of service?"

Tasha's lips twisted into a predatory snarl. "You thought you could kill me, you sniveling weasel?"

There was a moment's hesitation before he responded. "Ms. Levi, I assure you that was never my intention."

"You lied to me from the start. About what happened to my father—about *everything*."

"We should meet—"

"Guess where I'm sitting right now, Crisp?" Tasha lowered her voice, whispering fiercely. "At the New York field office of the FBI. I just told several agents all about you and your little side business."

"What?" Crisp snapped. Kasey heard the panic in his tone. "I don't believe you. Even you wouldn't do something that idiotic."

"Wanna bet? I only called because I want you to know that I'm the one who brought you down. They've already frozen your Cayman Islands account. And they're putting a team together to come arrest your sorry butt now."

Tasha was channeling all of her hate into the call. Kasey prayed it was enough to convince Crisp. If he bought her act, then he would hopefully be checking his bank account online right this second. And he'd be in for a big surprise.

Danny and his hacker friends couldn't actually freeze Crisp's account or take any of the illicit money he'd stashed there. The bank's online security was way too hard to penetrate. So they did something much sneakier, using the bank's own security against it.

They knew Braxton Crisp's bank account number, so Danny created a program that attempted to charge thousands of dollars to his account from locations all around the world. All these transactions triggered the bank's security features. In order to prevent massive fraud, the system was designed to instantly freeze the account. All Crisp could see was that his money was frozen, but he had no idea the FBI had nothing to do with it!

"You stupid little snit," he snarled, all trace of civility gone. Evidently, he'd confirmed it.

Crisp had millions of dollars in that account, and now he couldn't touch one cent of it. "I'll kill you myself!"

"Not from a federal prison, you won't. You messed with the wrong girl, Crisp." Tasha ended the call abruptly, turning to Kasey. "You think he bought it?"

"Are you kidding? I bought it, and I knew it was a lie!" They both looked toward the shop window across the street.

The idea was to flush Crisp out and get him on the run. If he believed the FBI was coming to arrest him, he'd be desperate to get out of the country as quickly as possible. And of course, he'd take the leather journal with the ERC identities with him.

Jacqueline and Edward, the burly Native American man Kasey had run into outside the brownstone, were covering the rear entrance. The assumption was that Crisp would come out the back and they'd be there to take him down. If he happened to go out the front, Tasha would follow him until they could get around and help her.

Within moments, the Closed sign was flipped over in the front window. Crisp peeked out, then disappeared.

Tasha keyed the walkie. "He took the bait. Looks like he's heading your way."

Kasey and Tasha waited anxiously, feeling powerless.

"A Suburban just pulled up to the back door," Jacqueline reported with frustration. "At least three men. You'd think they're guarding the president, the way they have him surrounded. Change of plan—we'll have to follow by car, see where he goes."

Tasha was already standing, taking the walkie. "I'll head south, let me know which way they go."

She slammed through the swinging door and raced out to her BMW without a good-bye. Kasey deflated. The mission would carry on without her. She stood to go, but the waitress blocked the way.

"You ready for the check?"

"Right—sorry." Kasey dug in her pocket and pulled out a twenty-dollar bill. As the waitress left to make change, she glanced out the glass door. Kasey suddenly froze, not believing what she was seeing.

Across the street, Braxton Crisp was coming out of his store. He wore a fedora to cover his bald head and carried a weathered brown shoulder bag. Looking around nervously, he hurried up the block. The Suburban and all the men at the back must have been a decoy!

Kasey swung the front door open.

"Your change," the waitress called.

"Keep it!" Pulling out her phone to call Jacqueline, Kasey hurried through the midday crowds.

Braxton Crisp wasn't getting away.

CHAPTER
47

**HOUDALI,
LOVANDA, AFRICA**

*T*he mood in Liberty Plaza had transformed from subdued to euphoric.
As Anbo and Delilah launched into
another number, the crowd sang along and
danced. Sekhmet Technologies workers managed to unplug one of the giant screens, but
the others continued to show the concert.

Perched on a low wall, Ryan saw over everyone's heads. The police officers guarding the
prisoners appeared panicked and uncertain.
Throngs of revelers had cut off their access to
the gallows.

Across the plaza, Madame Buku watched
the chaos from the balcony. She yelled at a uniformed officer as she pointed to a screen. The

statue of the African warrior and the baby was easy to spot behind Delilah. Hopefully, that would pull the cops away to the park on the other side of town. Ryan searched for Laughlin, but didn't see him anywhere.

All at once, police officers began to hurry away. Lights flashed and sirens wailed as squad cars raced from Liberty Plaza. Ryan felt a rush of adrenaline—the plan was working.

Moments later, the prisoners were on the move again. Police ushered them back toward the bus, fighting their way through the increasingly restless crowd. One bystander reached out and attempted to grab Jaz's hand as she passed. An officer hit him with the butt of his rifle, knocking the man down.

"They're heading back to the bus," Ryan reported. He jumped off the ledge and followed, keeping out of sight. The officers yelled at the prisoners, urging them to move quickly. Jaz and the others lumbered along. Their chained hands and ankles made walking difficult.

The door to the battered old prison bus stood open and waiting. Caden sat behind the steering wheel dressed in the driver's uniform, hat pulled low so his face was less visible. They had duct-taped the unconscious driver's hands and feet, then dragged him behind the bushes so he was hidden from view. He'd wake up in a couple of hours with a terrible headache.

When the bus had arrived, only the driver and one guard escorted the prisoners. Hopefully, that wouldn't change now. Ryan's dad was hidden inside. He could take out one guard, but if more boarded, he'd be outnumbered and the job would be much harder.

Ryan crept as close as possible, poised to do whatever he could to help his father. The prisoners were shoved in, trying not to fall as they stumbled up the steep metal steps. The guard who arrived with them was the last to board. As soon as the door swished closed, all the police officers took off running for vehicles. Every available unit was being called to the park.

The bus started forward as Ryan watched anxiously. Steel bars over the windows made seeing inside difficult, especially in the dark. A sudden burst of light illuminated the interior as a loud *crack* rang out—a gunshot from the rifle!

Ryan charged forward, fearing the worst. As he reached the back bumper, the bus screeched to a stop. The door swished open once more and a body tumbled out. Ryan raced to it with dread . . . but it was only the guard, moaning from a blow to the head.

Dad poked his head out. "Let's go."

Ryan was flooded with relief, but then noticed his father looking beyond him in alarm. He whirled around. At the far end of the street, a white SUV peeled around the corner. Laughlin and his men sped toward them. Their high beams blasted the bus, spotlighting Ryan with intense white light.

"Get in!"

Ryan jumped aboard. "Those are Madame Buku's mercenaries."

Calm and focused, Dad thrust the guard's keys into Ryan's hands. "Get everybody unlocked." He turned to Caden. "Better let me drive."

Caden jumped out of the driver's seat, immediately rushing to the only female prisoner other than Jaz. This woman must be his wife. They hugged tightly for a brief moment before the bus lurched forward.

Ryan turned to the shocked prisoners. "Grab hold of something! It's gonna get bumpy."

As his father shifted the bus into gear and revved the engine, the bus picked up speed. Ryan knelt in front of Jaz, frantically unlocking her cuffs and shackles.

"My name's Ryan," he told her. "I'm a friend of Anbo and Delilah's."

"I saw them on the screens. The police know where they are!" She was terrified and on the run, but still worried about her friends. Ryan liked her instantly.

"They're gonna be fine. You all are."

Ryan didn't actually feel as confident as he sounded, but she didn't need to know that. As the bus gained speed, he moved on to the next prisoner.

"Ryan, make sure everybody stays low!" Dad yelled.

It flashed through Ryan's mind that, at this moment, they weren't just father and son. He and Dad were partners. And it didn't feel strange at all. In fact, it felt completely natural.

Then the first bullet shattered the back window and everyone screamed! Ryan and the others dropped to the floor.

Dad punched the gas, and the bus shot forward.

CHAPTER
48

**NEW YORK,
USA**

Kasey was less than half a block behind Braxton Crisp. She was careful to keep hidden behind other people, knowing Crisp would recognize her. He had turned off Columbus Avenue and was cutting across to Central Park West, clutching the brown shoulder bag tightly to his side. The way he was protecting it made Kasey think the leather journal was probably stashed inside.

"He's heading toward the park," Kasey reported to Jacqueline.

"Don't follow him in there," Jacqueline ordered. "We're coming around on 72nd—we're only a couple of minutes away."

"We could lose him by then. He'll disappear with all those names."

"Kasey, you've done an amazing job. But Crisp is a trained operative. Keep your distance. We're turning onto Central Park West now."

There was a big crowd, so Kasey risked getting a little closer as Crisp crossed the big boulevard that bordered Central Park. When they reached the other side, he suddenly stopped and raised his arm. He was hailing a cab. Crisp wasn't heading to the park at all. He'd crossed to Central Park West so he could get a taxi heading uptown instead of downtown. Jacqueline and Edward were coming from the wrong direction—they wouldn't be able to follow him!

A yellow cab cut across traffic to the curb. As it arrived, Crisp let go of the shoulder bag and reached for the back door handle. If he got inside that taxi, they might lose him forever. He'd go right back to selling all the names of the ERC members to the highest bidders.

Kasey reacted instinctively. She charged forward and grabbed the strap of the shoulder bag. Crisp was caught off guard as she yanked the bag from his shoulder. She took off running as he whirled around.

"Hey! Stop—thief!" Crisp was right behind her, already giving chase.

Kasey dodged between people on the sidewalk. She glanced back and saw Crisp catching up. He might be older, but he was in good shape.

Park benches lined the low stone wall that surrounded Central Park. Kasey stepped up on one and used it to leap over the wall. A young kid wearing headphones yelped in surprise as she sprang past him.

Kasey landed and looked back. Crisp didn't slow down, jumping the wall easily. She scurried through the trees and brush. Carrying the shoulder bag made it hard to run.

Kasey darted across the jogging path and tried to cut around a tree, but her foot snagged on a root. She tripped, tumbling to the ground. The bag's flap opened and the contents spilled everywhere.

Crisp caught up, his eyes latching instantly onto the leather journal that now lay on the ground. Kasey snatched it up, prepared to run once more.

"I'd hate to have to shoot you, little girl." Crisp had produced a gun—one of the antique weapons from his shop. An old German Luger like the Nazis used. "But I will if you don't give me that."

Kasey clutched the book to her chest, looking around for help. No one was close enough to see what was happening, but they'd hear her if she screamed.

Crisp stepped forward, pulling back the hammer on the gun and preparing to fire. "Give me the journal!"

"Kasey, run!" From behind the tree, Tasha appeared. She barreled into Crisp, bear-hugging him with both arms. They fell with a thud as a shot rang out. Tasha rolled to the side and shouted, "Get that book out of here!"

Kasey ran as people reacted to the gunshot, screaming and hiding. She emerged onto one of the wide streets that meandered through the park, but jerked back as a car honked. Not paying attention nearly got her run over!

Behind her, Kasey saw Tasha and Crisp trade blows. Tasha knocked him to the ground, then advanced. Crisp twisted around and fired once more. The shot hit Tasha in the stomach and she doubled over.

"Tasha!" Kasey was horrified as the young woman fell to the ground. Crisp got back to his feet and continued his pursuit of Kasey.

She dashed across the street and suddenly knew exactly how she could make sure Braxton

Crisp never got those names back. Running alongside the street was the Central Park Lake, a huge body of water that was an oasis in the middle of the city. A mother picked up her child and hurried away as Kasey rushed toward the shoreline.

"Stop!"

Crisp approached the street, gun aimed at Kasey. She didn't hesitate. Treating the leather journal like a Frisbee, she flung it as far as possible. The journal sailed through the air, pages flapping in the wind, then landed with a splash.

"No!" Crisp appeared deranged as he ran forward. But his entire focus was on the journal, so he never saw the truck hurtling along West Drive. The truck driver slammed on the brakes, but there was no way to stop in time. The vehicle hit Crisp with a bone-shattering impact.

The driver leaped out to check on Crisp. Kasey realized she was hyperventilating and took a couple of deep breaths. She had to keep it together. Tasha needed help.

As people rushed toward the accident, Kasey made her way back across the street. She was relieved to discover Jacqueline already kneeling over Tasha. There was a lot of blood. Jacqueline applied pressure to the wound as a bystander called 911. Tasha was pale and weak, but her eyes were open. She locked eyes with Kasey.

"The journal?"

Kasey tried to sound brave. "It's gone—destroyed. We did it."

"Nice."

The bystander hung up their call. "Ambulance is on the way. How is she?"

Somehow, Jacqueline managed to sound calm and cool. "I think she'll be fine." She turned to Kasey and said quietly, "You need to get out of here. Now."

Kasey nodded, then looked at Tasha. "Thanks."

Tasha grinned. "You heard Mama Bear—get lost."

Turning away, Kasey saw that a small crowd had gathered in front of the truck. A man placed a jacket over the body that lay sprawled on the road.

Braxton Crisp was dead.

Kasey walked away, trying hard to pretend she was just a normal girl out for a day in the park.

CHAPTER
49

**HOUDALI,
LOVANDA, AFRICA**

Ryan grabbed the back of a seat to keep from falling as the prison bus careened around another corner. Dad veered erratically back and forth, trying to make it hard for their pursuers to shoot out the bus tires. They'd been driving for several minutes, but the SUV didn't try to catch up or pass them.

"Why are they hanging back?" Ryan asked, speaking loudly enough to be heard over the roar of the engine.

"I don't know." Dad checked the side mirror, as confused as Ryan. "But we have to lose them before the transfer."

"How much farther is it?"

"Less than a mile."

There was no way this beat-up bus could outrun the SUV. It was a mountain of metal, though. If Laughlin and his men got too close, Dad could ram their vehicle and run them off the road. But Ryan guessed that's exactly why they were keeping their distance. All they had to do was follow and the old bus could never get away. Somehow, they had to shake the SUV.

"Everybody, down!" Dad yelled.

Through the front window, Ryan saw what had caused his father's urgency: At the end of this narrow street, two more white SUVs skidded to a stop, blocking the road. Car doors opened and men piled out, weapons aimed at the bus. Laughlin had been hanging back so his other units could get into position.

Ryan dropped to the floor as a hail of bullets hit the front window. Glass shattered and the prisoners screamed. They instinctively covered one another with their bodies.

"Dad?" Ryan was terrified his father had been shot. But Dad had ducked below the dashboard. He'd avoided the bullets, but he couldn't see out the window. Driving blind, he managed to keep his hands on the steering wheel and his foot on the gas.

"Hold on!"

The bus never slowed even as it jerked sideways. Ryan held on to the metal base of a seat, trying to keep from sliding across the floor.

The prison bus hit an SUV in an explosion of metal and shattering glass. For a moment, everything felt weightless, like the bus might actually tip over. Dad sat up, wrestling with the steering wheel as he attempted to regain control. Finally, the tires regained traction.

In the rearview mirror, Ryan saw his father's reflection. Blood smeared his forehead. "Did you get hit?"

Dad wiped the blood off his brow with a sleeve. "Just a glass cut—I'm okay." The wind whipped his face, making him squint as he glanced in the mirror. "One of them's down, but the others are coming fast!"

Ryan started to stand, but stopped as he spotted a metal box underneath the seat. He yanked it out, revealing a red cross emblazoned on the lid. Ryan opened the box. It was a roadside emergency kit. First aid supplies, neon-yellow safety vests, light sticks . . . and a bright orange flare gun. Ryan grabbed the gun and three flare cartridges.

Standing, he staggered down the aisle, holding on to the seats to keep his balance. He stepped over one of the prisoners as he made his way to a steel mesh screen that separated the front half of the bus from the rear. This was where the most dangerous prisoners were kept. Ryan fumbled with the guard's keys, trying to find one that would unlock the gate.

"Ryan, what are you doing?" Dad yelled from the front.

"Trying to buy us some time! How far to the transfer point?" A gold key slid into the lock and turned. Ryan flung open the gate.

"Two blocks," Dad reported. "But I can't stop with them on my tail."

"They won't be."

Ryan was jostled from side to side, but made his way to the back window. It had been shot out, leaving only the metal bars on the outside. The two remaining white SUVs were closing in fast as Ryan loaded one of the cartridges into the orange flare gun.

The lead SUV approached on his right. Two of Laughlin's men leaned out, aiming their weapons. They pointed low, preparing to blow out the tires.

Ryan stuck the flare gun out the back window. He squeezed the trigger and a blazing ball of red sparks burst from the muzzle. The flare was designed to travel high in the air, but this one only had to go several yards. Like a rocket, it blasted between the vehicles and right into the open window of the SUV.

A white-hot explosion of sparks filled the inside of the SUV. The shocked driver jerked the steering wheel in surprise and the SUV smashed into a parked car. The momentum spun it around across the street. The second SUV slammed into it, both vehicles skidding to a stop.

Men jumped out of the first SUV as the flare continued to ignite. The other vehicle backed up and started after them once more.

Ryan turned to the front. "Make the transfer, Dad!"

"You sure?"

"Yeah!"

As the prison bus turned the next corner, Ryan opened the flare gun and jammed another cartridge in. He aimed out the back window, waiting for the SUV to appear.

The bus pulled to the side and screeched to a stop. Up front, Caden opened the door. The prisoners rushed off to a waiting van. Lacey, whose brother was among the prisoners, sat with the engine running, ready to drive them away down an alley that led in the opposite direction. The original plan called for everyone to leave in the van, but that was impossible now. They needed to make sure Laughlin didn't know the prisoners ever got off.

Dad yelled down the length of the bus. "You need to get out, too!"

"I can't." Ryan saw the white SUV turning the corner behind them. He fired and the flare shot down the street like a guided missile. It hit their window with a shower of sparks.

The SUV swerved, scraping against a row of parked cars. Ryan snapped open the gun and put in his last cartridge as the bus jerked forward. The transfer was complete and they were moving again. As the bus barreled around the next corner, the centrifugal force knocked Ryan over.

Getting to his feet, he looked out the back window as the white SUV fishtailed around the corner. Good, they were still following. Hopefully, that meant Laughlin hadn't seen the prisoners get off. The van could get away and get everyone someplace safe.

The SUV got close enough that Ryan could

make out Laughlin in the passenger seat. He aimed his pistol at the same time that Ryan raised the flare gun for one last shot.

"No!" Dad cried.

Ryan looked over his shoulder just in time to see a pickup truck cut in front of them. The bus abruptly veered, throwing Ryan across the seats and into the metal wall. Knocked around like a rag doll, Ryan barely had time to register what was happening as the bus popped the curb, plowed through a streetlight, and crashed into the brick wall of a building.

CHAPTER
50

**HOUDALI,
LOVANDA, AFRICA**

L awrence hadn't felt so alive in years.

Thumping bass beats pulsed through his body. Lyrics he'd written long ago came back like half-remembered dreams. Emotions he'd kept tightly locked away—anger, joy, grief, outrage—came pouring out. Every move he made felt natural and right. This was who he was meant to be.

Nadia crossed in front of him, and he took her hand. She was radiant, a fighter from the streets more assured and poised than he would ever be. She had never forgotten that she was Delilah, a charismatic presence with the voice of an angel and a message of hope. She inspired him.

But the flashing lights and wail of sirens meant this concert needed to end. From the improvised stage they had created, Lawrence could see over the heads of the hundreds of people who had gathered. The crowd surrounded them on all sides, offering protection. As more police arrived, though, their situation was getting increasingly perilous. The cops were still far away, but the concert stage made them easy targets for a rifle.

Nadia's eyes met his, and he knew she felt the same. They had created as much of a distraction as they could. It was time to go. As the song ended, Lawrence stepped forward. The portable microphones and speakers his friends provided carried his message across the park.

"Brothers and sisters, we must say goodbye." The crowd rumbled its disappointment. "But Delilah and Anbo won't disappear. We'll continue to sing out as long as we can. Each of you has a voice just as powerful. If we raise them together and stand as one, anything is possible."

Nadia stepped beside him. "Until there is freedom in Lovanda, the music must never die!"

The crowd roared in agreement. Lawrence saw the police forcing their way through the throngs. Guiding Nadia in front of him, they took off in the opposite direction. A car was waiting at the far end of the park for their escape.

The floodlights their friends used to illuminate the concert shut off and pandemonium quickly reigned. People scattered in the dark, frustrating the swarms of officers who were arriving. A gunshot created even more disruption as everyone panicked and ran.

Continuing to move, Lawrence and Nadia changed their appearance the way John Quinn had taught them. Nadia swept her braids up under a hat. The traditional gown she wore dropped to the ground, leaving her in the tattered blouse and jeans hidden underneath. Lawrence pulled off his "Live Free or Die Tryin'" shirt. Under it was a plain white T. Adding a gray beanie and black-rimmed glasses gave him a very different look.

Using the crowd's mass exodus as cover, they slipped away into the night.

CHAPTER
51

**HOUDALI,
LOVANDA, AFRICA**

Ryan propped his father up, helping him walk on his twisted ankle. The bus crash had injured both of them. Ryan's right shoulder and hip were aching from where he'd been thrown into the seats. But at least he could still move. Dad grimaced with every painful step he took.

Within seconds of the crash, Ryan had rushed up front to check on his father. More blood was smeared across his face, but Dad ignored it.

"Get out of here—run."

He pulled the lever that opened the side door, urging Ryan to go. But Ryan had grabbed his arm and helped him stand.

"Not without you."

"Ryan—"

"Are we gonna argue or get out of here before they start shooting?"

They faced off for a moment, then John staggered up. The bus blocked the view from the street, so Laughlin couldn't see them exit. Ryan scanned the area, searching for an escape route. They were in an industrial part of town with little evening activity. Moonlight illuminated the hulking skeleton of a five-story building towering overhead. It was under construction and surrounded by fencing, but Ryan spotted an entrance. They had just made it inside the construction site when the mercenaries started shouting.

"They know we're gone," Dad said. "It won't take them long to find us."

"Feel like playing 'Chameleon'?"

His father's brow furrowed in confusion before he understood. "Chameleon" was a game they'd played when he was young. Like an amped-up version of "Hide-and-Seek." The goal was to hide in the last place someone would look. Ryan had been unbeatable once he learned the Golden Rule of Hiding: Always go up. Nobody looks up high.

"Find a good spot," Ryan said, taking off. "I'll draw them away."

Scaffolding had been erected up the side of the building. Ryan ran toward it, not looking back. He knew his dad would only try to stop him. Leaping up, Ryan grabbed the metal poles and started climbing. Scrambling hand over hand, he quickly passed the second floor and continued upward.

The third-floor windows hadn't been installed yet. Ryan jumped onto the wood plank that ran alongside the building and looked back down. His father was nowhere to be seen. Hopefully, he'd found somewhere safe to hide amid the machinery and construction materials.

"There!" At the entrance, Laughlin pointed up at him. Ryan spotted three additional men, all armed. The beam from an intense flashlight swept across the building until it found Ryan. Perfect—that should get them away from Dad. Ryan darted through the window opening into the pitch-black gloom as a bullet ricocheted off the side of the building.

Ryan waited several seconds, allowing his eyes to adjust to the dark. Down below, he heard Laughlin order one of his men to stay put and shoot anything that moved. That meant three guys were coming after him.

This floor was huge and only half-finished. Some walls built from concrete blocks had been completed. Others were still only aluminum frames and had plastic tarps hanging from them. Waving gently in the moonlight, the tarps had a ghostly glow.

Avoiding the equipment and debris, Ryan crossed the building. Maybe he could go out a window on the other side and avoid Laughlin completely? Making it across, he was disappointed to discover there was no scaffolding. So no way down.

Turning back, he noticed a square hole cut out of the floor. It was surrounded on all four sides by yellow caution tape and orange cones. Peering down, Ryan realized the hole went through each floor. Probably for an elevator shaft that hadn't been built yet. If he had a rope of some kind, he could slide down. But there was nothing in sight that he could use.

A door slammed open at the far end of the building.

"You shoulda stayed in the mines, lad." Laughlin's voice echoed in the silence. "Might've lived longer there."

Ryan looked around desperately. Even as

dark as it was, Laughlin would spot him eventually. The building was too open and exposed with no good places to hide. Maybe he could sneak back out the way he came in. But as he turned in that direction, he saw a man's silhouette as he stepped in front of the windows, blocking the way.

"I never did like kids much." Laughlin's voice echoed, getting closer. "But now you've really given me a reason to hate 'em."

He couldn't hide, so he needed to even the odds. As quietly as possible, Ryan picked up one of the orange cones around the elevator shaft. He ripped off the caution tape and circled the hole, stacking the cones together.

Hearing the movement, the mercenary by the windows headed his way, the outline of a submachine gun visible in his hands. Ryan tossed all the cones down the shaft and ducked behind a column. As he slipped out of sight, the cones hit the floor three stories down with a loud bang.

Boots slapped the concrete as the armed man charged toward the sound. But in the deep shadows, the square hole was now impossible to see. Ryan peeked out just in time to watch the man step right into the empty space, completely unaware.

"Aaaaahh!" His startled scream was abruptly cut off as he smashed to the ground below.

"Hinckley?" Another of the mercenaries advanced cautiously. Ryan recognized Reilly, Laughlin's second-in-command.

"My legs!" the man groaned. "I think I broke my legs . . ."

"Idiot." Reilly spun around as Ryan ducked back out of sight.

One down, two to go.

CHAPTER

52

**HOUDALI,
LOVANDA, AFRICA**

Reilly advanced slowly. His boots made almost no sound as he stepped closer to the concrete column.

Pressed flat, Ryan tried not to breathe. Nothing but wide-open space around him. Any second now, Reilly would spot him. He had to get the gun away before Reilly got a shot off.

A plastic trash can was the only thing within reach. Ryan grabbed the handle with both hands. The barrel of Reilly's gun appeared less than two feet from his hiding place.

With one swift movement, Ryan yanked the trash can up and swung it around. The gray bin arced through the air and smacked into Reilly with jarring force. His weapon was knocked away, clattering to the concrete floor. Reilly was stunned, but didn't fall.

Ryan tossed the trash can aside and brought his knee up into the mercenary's stomach. Reilly was a lot bigger than Ryan, but he'd use the man's size against him. Grabbing his jacket with both hands, Ryan jerked Reilly off-balance and sent him sprawling to the ground.

Ryan realized too late that the gun was now within Reilly's grasp. Before he could reach it, Ryan kicked the gun as hard as he could. Many years playing soccer—or *football*, as kids called the game in most of the countries where he'd lived—paid off. The weapon disappeared, lost in the shadows. Ryan turned to confront Reilly.

And came face-to-face with Laughlin's pistol.

"You just don't know how to stay down, do you?" Laughlin raised the gun. "That's why I usually prefer a more permanent solution to problems."

Out of nowhere, a figure slammed into Laughlin. The gun fired, missing Ryan by inches. *Dad!* Even with his injured leg, he'd come after Ryan.

The two men rolled along the floor. Dad grabbed Laughlin's gun hand and banged it against the concrete until he let go. Ryan was about to grab it when two arms wrapped around him from behind.

Reilly was pissed. "You want to fight dirty? I can fight dirty, too!"

Ryan felt the air *whoosh* out of his lungs as Reilly squeezed. Across from him, Laughlin and his father traded a couple of fast blows. Both men were experts at hand-to-hand combat. Dad saw Ryan struggling and jumped up.

But Ryan's street-fighting training kicked in automatically. He dropped into a squat and shifted his hips to the side. Lunging forward to loosen Reilly's grip, he jabbed a sharp elbow into the man's solar plexus.

"Drop!" Dad yelled.

Ryan had trained with his father all his life and responded to his command instantly. He slumped to the ground as Dad's foot whizzed right over his head. The roundhouse kick connected with Reilly's jaw, spinning him around. The impact on Dad's injured foot must have been excruciating, but it did the job. Reilly fell to the ground, out cold.

"Dad, look out!"

But the warning was too late. Laughlin sucker punched his father from behind. Ryan watched in horror as his dad fell. He grunted in agony as he landed on his hurt ankle. Laughlin stomped down hard, but Dad rolled out of his way.

Ryan leaped forward. He swung a punch at Laughlin, but the older man blocked the swing. He tried to knee him, but Laughlin deflected that, too. Ryan was outmatched and knew it. But he couldn't give up.

Laughlin backhanded him. Ryan's head snapped around and he tasted blood in his mouth. The swing had left Laughlin vulnerable, though, and Ryan took advantage. He tried a left hook and finally connected. Laughlin staggered away a couple of steps, shaking off the blow.

Laughlin's British cool was gone. He was furious, glaring at Ryan with contempt. "Time to end this."

Too late, Ryan realized that Laughlin was going for his dropped gun. He ran forward, knowing he'd never stop him in time. Laughlin scooped up the pistol.

"Ryan!"

Everything seemed to slow down. Out of the corner of his eye, Ryan saw his father fling something into the air. A length of pipe. Never breaking stride, Ryan snatched it midflight.

Laughlin aimed the gun—

Ryan swung the pipe like it was a Louisville Slugger—

Laughlin's finger started to squeeze—

As the pipe whipped around and smashed into his head!

Laughlin twirled in a complete circle, then dropped to the floor. Ryan prepared to strike again, but the mercenary wasn't moving. Laughlin was down for the count.

Dad staggered up onto his good leg. Ryan dropped the pipe and helped him stand.

"You okay?"

"Hurts." Which probably meant it was agonizing.

Ryan hugged him tight. Partially it was to help his father walk, but mostly it was just because he wanted to feel him close.

"Those were some nice moves, son."

"I learned from the best."

Dad looked down at Laughlin, then smiled. "Gotta tell you—after seeing that swing, I'm definitely looking forward to baseball season."

Together, they headed out.

CHAPTER
53

**FARAJI PROVINCE,
LOVANDA, AFRICA**

The plane's engine whined in the shadows. Danny stood alone at the end of the landing strip, staring into the distance. If he kept wishing hard enough, maybe he could make Ryan and his dad appear. So far, the road back to Houdali remained empty and dark.

Madame Buku would be outraged if she knew they were using her landing strip to fly out of Lovanda. Since no one was out here at night, they had the place to themselves. Unfortunately, if things went according to plan, she'd probably never even know they'd been here.

That was okay, though. Danny had a few other surprises in store for Madame Buku. By tomorrow morning, news outlets around the world would be getting digital copies of all her emails and correspondence. Everything Danny and his hackers could pull from her computer was going to be public knowledge. There were records of bribes, threats, and countless illegal financial transactions all over the world.

Madame Buku was gonna have some explaining to do.

Nadia stepped up beside him. "They'll make it."

"They have to," Danny said. He wouldn't let himself believe anything different. Lawrence put a hand on his shoulder, offering support.

Behind them, a small plane waited. The ERC pilot had arrived fifteen minutes ago, and Candace was with him now. They would fly the short distance to her home in Ethiopia, where they could then make their way back to New York. But no way was Danny getting on that plane without Ryan and Mr. Quinn.

"Someone's coming." Lawrence pointed to the horizon.

A lone pair of headlights sped toward the airfield. The vehicle was moving fast. Danny was excited—it had to be Ryan. But as it came closer, he recognized the white SUV and his excitement faded.

"Oh no. That's one of the trucks Madame Buku's thugs were driving."

Nadia didn't hesitate, grabbing his arm and pulling him toward the plane. "Run!"

But as he turned to follow, Danny spotted someone leaning out the passenger window waving both arms wildly. The headlights flicked twice in greeting as Danny finally recognized Ryan.

"It's them! They made it!"

Danny ran to his friend. When the SUV pulled to a stop, Ryan hopped out.

"You're okay?" Danny asked.

"A little banged up is all." He turned as Lawrence and Nadia joined them. "Everybody got out?"

"The plan worked perfectly," Lawrence assured him. "What happened with Jaz and the others?"

"They all got away. They should be safely out of the country in a few hours."

Nadia hugged him tightly. "Thank you!"

"A little help here?" Dad asked behind them.

Ryan pulled out of the embrace and hurried

around the SUV. Helping his father out of the vehicle, Ryan motioned for Danny to lend a hand. "Can you get the other side?"

Mr. Quinn couldn't put any weight on his leg, so Ryan and Danny served as his crutches. "Let's load up," Dad said. "It's time to go home."

"Actually, we won't be joining you."

Ryan stopped, looking at Lawrence and Nadia in disbelief. "What do you mean? You can't stay in Lovanda—it's too dangerous."

Nadia nodded. "For now, you're right. We'll take the back roads and join Jaz and our friends across the border. But this is *our* home."

Lawrence wrapped an arm around her waist protectively. "No more running. No more hiding. Our fight is here."

"Mr. Quinn, tell them this is nuts," Danny sputtered.

But Dad didn't argue. Instead, he held out his hand to Lawrence. "Don't hesitate to contact us if we can ever be of help."

"Thank you." The men shook hands, then Lawrence turned to the boys. "And thank both of you, too. Not sure how I can ever repay you."

Ryan smiled. "Just keeping making great music. That's all the thanks we need."

"John!" Candace yelled from the runway as

the plane's engine revved up. "We need to go!"

Ryan and Danny hugged Lawrence and Nadia good-bye, then once more supported Ryan's dad. They made their way to the Cessna, shuffling along as quickly as possible.

"You know, Mr. Quinn," Danny said, "not to brag, but I think me and Ryan are pretty good at this rescue stuff. You should really consider making us full-fledged ERC members."

Dad turned a steely gaze his way. "What I'm considering is grounding Ryan until he's twenty-five and telling your parents to do the same."

"Sure, that's one option. Or you could make us *honorary* ERC members! A compromise."

Ryan started to laugh as his father stammered, "It's not a club. We don't have honorary members."

"Oh, you don't? So then we'll just be full members?"

"What? No—that's not what I said."

Ryan grinned as they arrived at the plane. "You might as well just say yes, Dad. He'll keep bugging you 'til you do."

Mr. Quinn limped up the stairs. "I've been interrogated by agents from Russia, China, and Pakistan. I can handle Danny."

The moment he disappeared into the plane,

Danny turned to Ryan. "We've got the whole trip back to change his mind. Think we can do it?"

"No doubt," Ryan said. "When we work together, we're virtually unstoppable."

The boys high-fived, then climbed aboard.

CHAPTER
54

**NEW YORK,
USA**

EIGHT DAYS LATER . . .

The crowd in Times Square was ready to party. A big clock on top of the Toshiba building said it was only a few minutes to midnight. Everyone was bundled up against the cold, but that didn't stop them from having fun. Ryan resisted a slight feeling of claustrophobia. He'd never been around this many people at once in his life. But with Kasey on one side and Danny on the other, at least he was surrounded by friends.

They were celebrating New Year's Eve NYC-style. Drew and Kasey's dad were here also, along with her two oldest brothers. It was so busy, they'd had to get here hours ago just to make sure they had a place to stand. Fortunately, the Stieglitz men were all giants—Kasey's two college-age brothers were even taller than Drew! They formed a wall, keeping the younger trio from being shoved around too much.

"So after the Quinns dropped me off with my family, I went on and on about how amazing the camping trip was." Danny was midway through a story, his voice already hoarse from yelling over the chatter of thousands. "I told my parents I didn't miss my cell phone or laptop at all."

"And they believed you?" Kasey asked.

"Yeah, and it totally backfired." Danny looked to Ryan, who grinned. He knew how this story ended. "Since I loved it so much, they signed our whole family up for a camping trip. An entire week with just my parents and my sisters! And no internet! I'm gonna die."

As they laughed, Ryan remembered how happy Danny had been to be back home. He might pretend to be annoyed by his little sisters, but Ryan knew the truth. When he saw Analyn and Lilibeth, Danny had hugged them both until they finally pulled away and ran off squealing. Danny adored his family, even if he didn't always admit it.

After leaving Lovanda, they had barely made

it back for Christmas Eve. Christmas was a big deal in Filipino culture, and Ryan's mom had promised Danny's parents that he wouldn't miss it. Luckily, they had arrived just in time.

Standing in the Santiagos' living room, Ryan had marveled at how effortlessly his mom talked about their "camping trip." The anxiety and stress she'd been feeling for days was completely concealed. She was just a regular mom telling funny stories about their vacation. He understood now that she had been lying his whole life to keep him safe. She'd become really good at it.

Over Christmas and the next few days, Ryan had spent a lot of time with his parents. Mom was upset with Dad for letting Ryan and Danny take part in the rescue mission in Lovanda. But Dad held his ground, saying the boys had done great. They'd rescued Lawrence and Nadia and saved five innocent people from being executed. Plus, Danny's release of Madame Buku's personal records had exposed her illegal financial activities all over the world. The people of Lovanda were outraged, leading to giant protests fueled by several Anbo and Delilah pop-up concerts across the nation. The government ended up with no choice but to order Madame

Buku's arrest. She was now sitting in a jail cell awaiting trial.

Mom had to admit that Kasey had also handled herself remarkably well. Without her help, Braxton Crisp would still be selling ERC identities. Ryan's parents weren't convinced the kids should take part in ERC activities yet, but he was slowly wearing them down.

To no one's surprise, Tasha Levi had disappeared from the hospital and not been seen since. Dad was hurt and angry when he learned about her betrayal. He considered Tasha part of his extended family and had always looked out for her, especially after her father's death. He never even suspected she was keeping such a huge secret from him.

Which made him even more insistent there be no more secrets inside their own family. Mom and Dad were obviously relieved at being able to finally open up to Ryan about his history. He learned a little more about his birth, though they didn't know much more than Dad had already told him.

A couple of days ago, though, they had invited Principal Milankovic over. Seeing his principal sitting in their kitchen felt odd at first. But Ludo Milankovic was Ryan's only connection to his birth parents. Having watched Nina grow up, Milankovic had lots of great stories about her. She was adventurous and loved to ride horses and play sports. Ryan enjoyed listening, but couldn't help feeling sad that he never got to know her.

Before he left, Principal Milankovic gave Ryan a photo of Nina and his birth father at their wedding. It looked like a huge celebration, and both the bride and groom were beaming. Theirs was a great but tragic love affair, Milankovic said. But he could see that the conversation was taking a toll on Ryan and suggested they save that story for another day. When he was gone, Ryan looked at the picture for a long time.

It would take a while to sort out his feelings, and he was okay with that. Mom and Dad would be there with him every step of the way. They were his family. He knew he could count on them no matter what.

"Hey—Ryan Quinn, right?"

Ryan turned as someone tapped his shoulder. He didn't recognize the teenager in the red top hat with "Happy New Year" emblazoned across the front. He looked kind of like a young Mad Hatter.

"Yeah," Ryan answered. "Do we know each other?"

"I've just heard a lot about you around school." The kid was probably late teens and had a mischievous smirk. "Catch you in the new year, man!"

Ryan didn't remember seeing him at school. He was pretty sure he'd never seen him anywhere. As quickly as he'd appeared, the guy spun around and melted into the crowd. Within moments, he'd vanished.

"One minute, kids!" Kasey's father announced, diverting Ryan's attention. "Everybody ready?"

Kasey was on her toes, taking in the frenzied activity of Times Square. "I can't believe I'm finally getting to do this."

Danny leaned in close to Ryan. "You know, at the stroke of midnight, you're supposed to kiss her."

"What?" Ryan felt his stomach twist in a knot. "Here? In front of her dad and brothers?"

Danny made smooching sounds.

Drew leaned in, having heard them. "Kiss her and die."

"Five-four-three-two-one-Happy New Year!"

Ryan screamed along with everyone else as the night exploded in fireworks. Confetti canons shot into the air creating a snowstorm of colored paper. Music blared as the crowd broke out in a disjointed chorus of "Auld Lang Syne."

Ryan and Danny hugged. "Happy New Year!"

"This is gonna be the best year ever!" Danny yelled.

Ryan turned to Kasey, who was laughing and spinning in a circle. Her wild hair was littered with blue and green paper. Her eyes sparkled as they found Ryan's.

Before he even registered what was happening, Kasey leaned in and kissed him. It was his first real kiss, and Ryan prayed he wasn't screwing it up. Drew and Kasey's other brothers were probably glaring at him. Danny would tease him mercilessly. But who cared?

He was kissing the prettiest girl he'd ever met in the middle of Times Square on New Year's Eve!

Maybe this really would be the best year ever.

EPILOGUE

**NEW YORK,
USA**

Through the jubilant crowd, Markus watched Ryan kissing the girl. He looked so happy. Without a care in the world.

Markus pulled off the ridiculous red top hat he'd been wearing. Tossing it to the ground, he forced his way through the mass of bodies. These Americans were so spoiled and decadent. He couldn't wait to get out of here.

Following Ryan and his friends to Times Square was dangerous. Actually going up and speaking with him was even riskier. But Markus lived for danger. He craved risk. And besides, he'd been so curious to finally meet the boy he'd heard about all his life.

Finally making it out of the madness of the celebration, Markus took out his cell phone. He dialed an international number and waited for it to connect. It was a private number, known to only a handful of people. Markus was proud to be among them.

"*Ya?*"

"Uncle Janos, it's me." Markus was always extremely respectful with his uncle. Janos Balazar ruled Pelskova with a firm hand. Even from his family, he demanded submission.

"Did you find Kostya?"

"I did. I've seen him myself."

There was a long pause on the other end. "Very good, Markus."

Markus swelled with pride. He couldn't recall ever receiving a compliment from his uncle.

"What do you want me to do?"

"Kostya Balazar belongs in Pelskova," Uncle Janos said. "I want you to bring him home."

TO BE CONTINUED . . .